Get **more** out of libraries

Please return or renew this item by the last date shown.

You can renew online at www.hants.gov.uk/library

Or by phoning 030

 Hampshire
County Counc

D1513854

C015981150

Pretty Thing

Jennifer Nadel

corsair

CORSAIR

First published in Great Britain in 2015 by Corsair, an imprint of
Little, Brown Book Group
1 3 5 7 9 10 8 6 4 2

Copyright © Jennifer Nadel, 2015

The moral right of the author has been asserted.

*All characters and events in this publication, other than
those clearly in the public domain, are fictitious
and any resemblance to real persons,
living or dead, is purely coincidental.*

A CIP catalogue record for this book
is available from the British Library.

ISBN: 978-1-47211-398-6 (paperback)
ISBN: 978-1-47211-399-3 (ebook)

Typeset by SX Composing DTP, Rayleigh, Essex
Printed and bound in Great Britain by CPI Group (UK) Ltd., Croydon, CR0 4YY

Papers used by Little, Brown are from well-managed forests
and other responsible sources.

MIX
Paper from
responsible sources
FSC® C104740
www.fsc.org

Corsair
An imprint of
Little, Brown Book Group
100 Victoria Embankment
London EC4Y 0DY

An Hachette UK Company
www.hachette.co.uk
www.littlebrown.co.uk

For Jack, Theo, Arlo and, of course, Roo

NOW

It might have been different if both things hadn't happened on the same day.

But, there's no way of finding out. No rewind or delete buttons in real life.

Where does the story start? Pick a point, any point.

I'll pick me and Mary-Jane sitting in a bath. We're toddlers. Splashing and shrieking. Mary-Jane's chubby fingers reaching out to clasp my arm. Beside the bath our mothers. Best friends. Mine has a Martini in one hand. Her miniskirt has ridden up. There's a flash of her knickers showing.

Jump forward five years. We're standing on the doorstep of Mary-Jane's cottage. We're both draped in net curtains and wearing tutus. When we grow up we're going to be brides. Mary-Jane has borrowed her mother's lipstick and has left a scarlet kiss on my cheek.

Fast-forward to 1976. The year of the longest, hottest summer since records began. I'm wearing my ripped Levi's and my white cheesecloth shirt. I've decided it's time to fall in love. Mary-Jane isn't with me. It's the year the two things happened. One to Mary-Jane. One to me. Before long everyone started seeing coincidences. Everyone, that is, except me.

THEN

1976

Chapter 1

I didn't like lying, but I had to.

Dad gave me no choice. He'd have killed me if he knew where I was going. He was terrified I'd turn out like Mum and lose my reputation. And his, all over again.

That meant pubs were out of bounds. So was using the phone and generally doing anything I wanted to.

I waited for my chance to sneak out.

Dad was watching the news or rather ranting at the TV.

On the screen, people were marching and banging drums. It was another anti-nuclear protest. We were all about to die in some horrific holocaust courtesy of the cold war and the arms race.

'Bloody hippies. Need a good bath,' said Dad.

Dad thought any bloke with long hair was a good-for-nothing. His idea of casual was to wear tweed. I wish I'd been born ten years earlier so I could've been a hippy. But I didn't say so as Dad would've accused me of picking a fight.

He poured himself another tumbler of Johnny Walker.

I could smell his breath from across the room. The IRA could've used him as an incendiary device. He'd have exploded if I'd lit a match.

'Night, Dad.' I shoved my books in my school bag so he'd think I was taking them upstairs to bed.

'Revision,' Dad slurred. 'Revision maketh man.'

'Of course, Dad. Only I'm a woman.'

I waited for ten minutes at the end of Mary-Jane's lane but she didn't come.

Coward, I thought, as I pumped my bike pedals up the hill to find her.

Mary-Jane lived in one of those whitewashed cottages with dark Tudor beams and roses climbing all over it. 'A chocolate box house' Mum had always called it. Peeking through the leaded window I could see Mary-Jane sitting at the kitchen table with her parents playing Mousetrap. They looked so perfect they were a cliché.

What was it Tolstoy said about happy families? They were all the same. Only the unhappy ones got to be different. Great consolation prize. Frankly, I'd have taken normal any day.

Mary-Jane opened the door. She had waist-length blonde hair, a nose she thought was too small and was skinny like a sapling. She'd wanted to be a ballet dancer but she'd already grown too tall.

'Becs,' she said, flinging her arms around me. Her hair smelt of Silvikrin.

'You're not ready.'

'What?' she said and then, 'Oh God, Becs, I'm so sorry.

I forgot. We're just about to have supper. But there's loads. Stay. It's shepherd's pie.'

'Darling, do come and join us,' Mary-Jane's mum shouted from the table. She was a perfect replica of her daughter only taller and blonder.

'I can't,' I mumbled.

Mary-Jane followed me back out as I picked my way across the dry grass to my bike.

'I'll try to come,' she said but I knew she didn't mean it.

'You always do this,' I said as I cycled off. 'If you're not careful you'll end up on the shelf.'

I propped my bike against the wall of the pub. I'd painted lime green and shocking pink swirls all over it. Dad said it looked common, which made me like it all the more.

Bits of gravel bit into the soles of my feet as I picked my way across the car park. I never wore shoes unless I had to. They were bourgeois, like Dad.

The stench of stale bitter hit me as soon as I opened the door. The George was heaving. From the juke box in the corner, Barry White was crooning *You're the first, my last, my everything*.

I scanned the room. None of the others had arrived yet. Mary-Jane should have been there. Now I was left standing all alone in the middle of the packed pub like a giant pimple. Usually in this sort of situation, I'd have gone and hidden in the loos, but for some reason, maybe because I was cross with Mary-Jane, I decided to get a drink.

The barmaid ignored me. She was too busy flicking her Farrah Fawcett hair at some bloke at the other end of the bar.

I watched them in the mirror. I'd never seen him before. He was well over six feet with thick dark hair that stuck out in all directions as if someone had just ruffled it. His denim jacket was battered in all the right places and it looked like he was wearing a Grateful Dead T-shirt.

Sal would freak when she saw him. Sal was the one who'd got me into pubs. She was hard and cool with a real leather biker's jacket and lots of older brothers. I couldn't believe it last term when she'd said we were best friends. I didn't dare tell her I already had one; Mary-Jane had been mine since nursery.

Someone put 'Imagine' on the juke box, which always made me cry on account of how much better things could be. For instance, I could not have red hair and be stringy and awkward and put boys off by talking about books. And Dad could stop drinking and get over Mum and stop being so pompous and mean. Reality was really overrated.

The barmaid was still drooling over the bloke, leaning forward across the counter so her T-shirt flopped low. I leant forward too so I could hear what he was saying.

'Buzz off,' she hissed at me, which made me blush the deep red that rotting strawberries go. I pretended to look for something in my pocket.

'I'll take a pint of your Carlsberg,' I heard the guy order. His voice was deep and slightly nasal, his accent the kind Dad would definitely not approve of. And then he said, 'And one of whatever the young lady would like.'

I looked around. There were only men at the bar. A knot were jostling to get served and in front of them a row of regulars perched on their stools staring solemnly into their pints as if they were oracles.

'Well?' the barmaid said, giving me a fake smile. 'What would the young lady like?' She stressed the word young in a way that wasn't nice.

By this point I was flustered. Normally I was invisible to boys.

'Vodka and lime,' I mustered, which was dumb as according to Sal's oldest brother, Wayne, who was a copper, you should never order spirits until you'd sussed out whether the landlord minds that you're underage.

But the barmaid just flicked her hair at the guy and pulled a glass off the shelf. I watched her measure out the Vladivar and then daub it with thick green syrup. I was trying to avoid looking at the bloke in case I blushed again but then suddenly he was beside me.

'Bracken,' he said. He was much taller than me and older. Old enough to have been a real hippy. I tipped my head back to meet his gaze. His eyes were brown. Not normal brown, but deep dark brown the colour of rain-soaked wood.

'Bracken,' he said again, 'as in fern.'

The skin around his eyes crinkled into a smile and it took me a moment to realize I was meant to tell him my name.

'Rebecca,' I said, trying to sound grown-up. Becs was what everyone actually called me but it didn't feel nearly sophisticated enough. I wished I'd been christened with the name of a romantic heroine, like Zelda or Zuleika.

Bracken took my arm and led me away from the bar. 'She was a fake, wasn't she?' he said, glancing back at the barmaid. 'Thought she might throw you out. How old are you anyway?'

I hesitated, not wanting to put him off.

'Fifteen.' I didn't have the guts to lie.

'You've got an old soul, though. I can tell.' He smiled again.

And then suddenly we were chatting. Like we were old friends, chatting so easily I'd forgotten to be shy or mute like I normally was if someone I liked tried to talk to me. Bracken told me about the garage he'd just opened and how he still lived with his mum on account of not wanting her to be lonely.

'What's your biggest sadness?' I asked, sounding much more confident than I was. I'd read once that you can tell whether someone's right for you by their sadnesses.

'That's heavy.' His face grew kind of serious and for the first time our conversation just dried up.

I downed my vodka. I always said the wrong thing. Maybe I should invent an urgent reason to leave, like a chip pan on the stove. But before I could do anything he took my empty glass and went back to the bar and ordered me another, pulling a crisp ten pound note from a smooth leather wallet to pay for it. None of the boys our age had tenners, let alone wallets.

He handed me what looked like a double. 'I guess it was Dad,' he said. 'My sadness. Yes, it was Dad leaving. I was four.'

Snap, I thought. Only I was nine when Mum left.

A strobe light suddenly flickered into action and a DJ introduced himself over a crackly mic. People started to dance on the raised area to the right of the bar. I felt the vodka threading its way through my veins. Ice cold then warm.

The DJ put on 'You Sexy Thing' and I let out an involuntary squeal. Mary-Jane and I loved this song. Especially the chorus, *I believe in miracles*. I mouthed quietly letting my hips gently sway.

The vodka must've made me tipsy because before I knew it I'd started to dance as well, started to twirl and spin around the floor. I didn't decide to, it just happened. My arms stretched out and my white cheesecloth shirt swirled out behind. Normally I'd only ever have danced like this with Mary-Jane.

I closed my eyes, hoping it looked like I was concentrating on the music but really I was hoping I could magically make myself sexy and grown-up enough for this man. When I opened my eyes again Bracken was there looking at me and smiling, which made me happy and shy at the same time.

Chapter 2

When 'Nights in White Satin' started playing Bracken stepped onto the dance floor. He didn't ask. He just came right up and grabbed me. Before I knew it we were slow dancing. He held me close. So close I was worried he'd feel my heart beating and know I wasn't experienced, that I'd barely ever danced with anyone before.

He smelt of too much aftershave and there was another funny smell mixed in that I couldn't name. I didn't really like the smell but I liked the way he was holding me, the way his arms folded so tightly around me that I had no choice but to rest my head against his chest. I liked the way he felt – strong and certain. Like a nuclear bomb could drop and I'd still be okay.

I liked the way he didn't give me a choice.

Boys our age always gave us a choice, which was dumb and a trap because you could never say yes unless you didn't care about looking slutty. Bracken didn't bother with that. He bent his head down so it rested on top of mine. We were turning round. Not fast. Just fast enough so that it counted as dancing. I closed my eyes. My head was spinning and as I leant against him it felt like I was melting.

When the track was about halfway through one of his hands started to slide ever so slowly down my back. So slowly it was almost like it wasn't happening at all. But it was. His hand was reaching down my back inch by gradual inch until it paused just above my bum. Then he started to push me, gently but firmly, even closer to him. At the same time one of his legs started to move ever so softly so that it was in between mine. I wondered whether I ought to say 'no' or 'stop' but I didn't. I didn't want him to stop.

Pretty soon we'd stopped dancing, we were just rocking slightly. My eyes were still closed, I didn't want to know if anybody was watching us. I wanted there to be just us. His leg slid further so it was right between mine, pushing against where my legs joined. Very slowly his leg started to move up and down and his hand moved so that it was right on my bum and I couldn't escape the motion of his leg. The seam of my jeans started biting into me. It hurt a bit but I didn't mind: there was another feeling that was much stronger. No one had ever held me like that or made me feel that way before. I wondered if this was what falling in love felt like.

The song ended but neither of us moved. We just stood there locked together. Eventually Bracken leant down and whispered, 'I think we'd better go outside.'

He didn't wait for an answer. He just started walking and I followed. On the way out I saw Sal leaning against the cigarette machine with her leather jacket and her new Brutus flares on. No sign of Mary-Jane. Guess she must have stayed at home. Typical. Sal stared at me like she was cross or maybe just puzzled. I didn't speak to her as we walked past. We'd all agreed that we could ignore each other if we met a boy and it wouldn't count. Not that Bracken was a boy. He was a real man. Sal was probably jealous.

Outside the sky was dark velvet, the moon a fragile new-born sliver of light. The car park was deserted. Everyone must have been still inside trying to get one more in before last orders. Bracken walked. I followed. The gravel didn't hurt my feet any more. He led me to the furthest corner and stopped in front of a white van. On its side in large black letters was written 'S. Bracken Autos'. When I caught up with him he put his hands on my shoulders and swung me round so my back was leaning against the van. The metal was steely cold through my shirt.

Then with the streetlight behind him and behind that the new moon he bent down and put his mouth to mine. Our lips touched, just for a moment. Then he took a step back and stared at me very hard, like he was trying to work something out.

After what felt like forever he moved back to me and put his lips on mine again. This time he let them stay there and before long I felt his tongue against my lips pushing deeper and deeper into my mouth. I kissed him back, or tried to, not sure exactly what I was meant to do. His tongue felt rough and large and wide. Just as it was starting to feel like it was okay he stopped. Taking a step away again he just stood there staring at me.

I must've done it wrong. Maybe I tasted disgusting or my tongue was just the wrong size or shape. His lips, wet with my saliva, curled up into a bow. There was a slight lopsided twist to the way he smiled that made it almost look like a snarl.

'I'd better take you home,' he said and fiddled in his pocket to pull out a large clump of keys. 'Don't want to do anything I might regret.'

He opened the van door and I thought about my bike leaning against the wall and climbed in.

The lane shimmered silver in the headlights. Neither of us said anything. It was like there wasn't anything that needed to be said. When we got to my lane I told him to drop me by the phone box so Dad wouldn't hear the engine.

'Just a minute,' Bracken said as I started to climb out.

He reached across and took a strand of my hair in his fingers.

'It's gorgeous,' he said. 'Red's my favourite.'

Then he kissed me lightly on the lips and I was out of the van and he was gone.

I didn't sleep that night. I lay awake with the bedroom curtains open so I could see the night sky.

It felt like something very significant had happened. Something I'd been waiting for all my life. Something I'd read about but never known. I replayed the evening over and over and finally got lost in the moment where he held me while we danced. I put my hand where his leg had been and tried to make the feeling come back.

It was only in the morning as I got up for school that I realized he hadn't asked how to get hold of me. I might never see him again.

Chapter 3

My next-door neighbour Pete was already at the bus stop. He ignored me and for once I didn't care. I had Bracken to think about. I pulled a copy of *Tess of the D'Urbervilles* out of my bag and pretended to read it.

Every morning Pete and I stood in silence on either side of the red pillar box as if we were on sentry duty waiting for the bus. I could hear his fingers drumming out a rhythm on his thigh. I'd had a massive crush on him ever since he'd suddenly arrived halfway through last term. Nobody knew what he was doing at the comp. He was way too posh and cool.

'You never know, he might be one of those guys who likes red hair,' Sal had said. 'Some guys do, otherwise there wouldn't be any of you left. You'd just have died out.'

But the truth was he either hadn't noticed I existed or worse still he'd guessed I fancied him. I was his only fan. Everyone else thought he was stuck up because he'd been to boarding school and had a house with a swimming pool and two drives.

At our school being posh was far worse than being brainy or putting your hand up. I'd never told them I was meant to go away to school myself; it would have been social suicide.

On the morning I was due to leave for boarding school I'd taken my bike lock and chained myself to the bed, like a suffragette. Dad was furious, he said I was throwing my life away. He just didn't understand that I couldn't leave home in case Mum came back to get me. And even if she never came, home was where I could feel Mum's presence. Sometimes I reckoned I could actually hear her voice like its echo was trapped in the bricks. It was one of those background sounds that you only notice if you really concentrate, like the sound a bird makes when it lands on a branch.

A plume of smelly black smoke filled the lane as the bus lurched into sight. It should've been scrapped years ago but the Council was legally obliged to collect us as we lived more than three miles from school. Sometimes when it was snowy, which was hardly ever as we lived in Essex not Kathmandu, it didn't come at all and we got to stay at home.

The bus was always late on account of Les the driver not wanting to leave anybody behind. Everyone took advantage, pretending they'd forgotten their gym kits or just generally walking as slowly as they could to try to make the bus late enough to miss Assembly.

Les winked at me as I got on and offered me a humbug from the huge plastic jar he kept on the floor by the gear stick. He had a soft spot for me, partly because of Mum and partly because although I hung out with the trouble makers he knew I'd never cause trouble myself. I was way too scared of what Dad would do.

As usual Elvis was blaring out of his tinny tape deck. We'd beg him to play something else like the Stones or Bowie or even the Beatles but he was an old rocker, he'd just tap his finger against his nose and say, 'Driver's choice.'

Halfway down on the left was where I always sat. Marion and Pen were already there but I couldn't tell them about Bracken until Sal was there. Sal was the one whose opinion counted and she hated not to hear things first.

It took forever for the bus to bounce its way to her village past large fields of flat, boring farmland and clusters of quiet cottages where nothing, absolutely nothing, happened. Until last night I'd thought things could only happen elsewhere. Life was something I heard about on my crackly radio under the bed sheets at night. Not something that actually happened here to me. Sal would freak when I told her and want to know every last detail.

As soon as Sal got on it was obvious there was something wrong. For starters she didn't stop to flirt with Les. Sal and Sarah Slater always flirted with Les. Sarah Slater was a 36B and always undid an extra button on her shirt to try to tempt him. One time she actually sat on his lap and bounced up and down so that her boobs were practically in his face. Afterwards she'd said he'd got excited and it was disgusting and he was a filthy old man, but nobody believed her. Les just wasn't like that.

Sal set her face to 'serious' as she walked up to join us. She wanted to be an actress and so lived like she was in constant dress rehearsal. Always arranging her features to convey a serious emotion.

'You lot heard about Mary-Jane?'

'She's not here,' answered Marion.

'Exactly.' Sal shoved Penny up so she could squidge onto our row. Her hair was scraped back in a leather barrette with her flicks left curving out to each side, like short shiny curtains. 'Want to know why Mary-Jane's not here?'

'Not really,' said Dave, Pen's little brother, from the row in front. He always sat there in his filthy camouflage jacket eavesdropping from behind his *Socialist Daily Worker* paper.

'Shut up. No one asked you,' said Pen.

'Go on, Sal. Spit it out.' I wanted her to get on with it so I could tell her about Bracken.

'It's top secret,' she stage whispered. 'You've got to promise not to tell. Wayne heard it at the police station.'

We all nodded obediently.

'It happened last night on her lane. This van just pulled up beside her.' She paused to smooth her hair back and make sure we were all listening. 'Anyway, this white van pulled up beside her with an old guy in it. Once he was level with her he rolled his window down and asked her how to get to the Mill Pond.'

'So?' said Marion.

'So, shut up or I won't effing tell you.'

'So-rr-y,' said Marion.

'So, once she'd stopped and turned to tell him she looked into the window and his trousers were round his ankles.'

'What do you mean?' asked Marion, who was so unbelievably slow that she still liked Jimmy Osmond.

'His trousers were round his ankles,' Sal repeated but by that time she'd totally forgotten to keep her voice down and was virtually shouting. 'He was displaying himself.'

'Poor Mary-Jane,' I said.

'Oh my God,' shrieked Pen, who was normally unflappable.

Marion leant across. She always had a layer of fuzzy white gunk over her protruding top teeth. 'Why?' she asked.

Pete let out a snort from the row behind. He always sat somewhere near us instead of down the back with the other boys.

'Because,' Sal lowered her voice again, 'he was touching his thing. He opened his door so she could see everything. She didn't have a choice. There wasn't time for her to look the other way.'

By then we were all silent.

I hoped Sal was making it up.

She continued slowly and deliberately. 'That's not all. He grabbed her hand and he made her touch it.'

Marion and Pen started screaming 'pervert' and 'gross' and pretty soon the entire bus was listening to her telling the story again only this time she was somehow making it sound even worse.

It's my fault, I thought. I made her come to the pub.

Then the bus hit a pothole and someone shouted 'bundle' so all the boys pretended to fall on top of the girls.

'Sit down!' bellowed Les from the front. 'You lot sit down and shut up.'

I had a sick feeling in the pit of my stomach – all I could see was Mary-Jane's long blonde hair and someone grabbing hold of it.

'She was wearing her capped-sleeve Etam T-shirt,' Sal was saying, 'you know, the one with the pink teddy bears on.'

'Men are all the same,' Pen said. She loved to pretend she knew it all but there was only one person any of us knew who'd actually done it. That was Sarah Slater's big sister Debbie, who'd got pregnant and was kicked out of school for it. She'd wanted to be a model, had her photos done and everything, and now she stacked shelves at the Spar.

'It's my fault,' I said. 'I made her come to the pub.'

'Don't be stupid,' snapped Sal. 'She'd never have been coming to the pub, not in a million years. What planet are you on?'

'She was probably just posting a letter or counting the stars or something,' said Pen, who could tell I was upset.

'Yeah probably,' I shrugged. But inside I knew. I knew it was my fault. Mary-Jane had never even snogged a boy properly; she was the last person this should've happened to.

I leant my forehead against the glass and watched the town slide into view. Row upon row of identical houses. I suddenly felt a million miles away from everyone and then I thought of Bracken. I imagined burying myself in his arms for protection and a warm fuzzy feeling crept up my body. It was good I hadn't told anyone about him. It was too private and too precious. It was my secret. Telling anyone would ruin it.

Chapter 4

After school I got off at the stop nearest The George. I stood in the car park for a moment. It was deserted like the stage after a show had finished.

I closed my eyes and imagined Bracken there, holding me, pressing me back against his van and kissing me. And then I felt weird and embarrassed. What would happen if he drove by now and saw me standing there thinking about him? I grabbed my bike and pedalled as fast as I could round to Mary-Jane's.

Her bedroom door was closed. It had been wonkily painted with a picture of an orange sun setting behind purple mountains. Her mum did it and her mum's an air stewardess for TWA, not an artist. Mary-Jane used to get hysterical when her mum travelled so, one weekend, her parents said they were going to make her a faraway place of her own right there in her bedroom. We were both allowed to help. In those days, after Mum went, I virtually lived with Mary-Jane.

Her dad rested a plank of wood between two ladders so he

could lie on his back. That's how Michaelangelo did the Sistine Chapel, he told us. And while he painted the ceiling dark blue with yellow stars, Mary-Jane's mum stencilled palm trees onto the walls and told him that if he'd been Leonardo, the Pope would have demanded his money back. We were given little brushes to do the colouring in. The room smelt of paint for weeks and Mary-Jane thought it was the coolest thing ever.

I pushed the door open. Mary-Jane was sitting on her bed with her long legs pulled up and her chin resting on her knees and her hair hanging down like a shield. She was staring straight ahead at the wall with the palm trees on, only she didn't look like she was seeing it.

'Mary-Jane,' I said but she just kept staring. I went over and sat on the bed in front of her. She lowered her face to avoid me. I bent my head down so that it was even lower than hers and then twisted it up to look at her.

'Hello,' I said in a silly voice that was meant to sound like a Clanger.

Mary-Jane closed her eyes and her face scrunched up as she started to cry.

'Oy, careful!' I said in my alien voice. 'I'm getting wet. You're dripping on me. Not nice.'

Before I knew it we were both laughing and it was like it always was. I hugged her and as she hugged me back I noticed how bony she'd got. She'd been losing weight ever since she was told she was too tall to go to ballet school.

'I don't want to talk about it,' she said before I could ask her. And then, 'Does everybody know?'

'I don't think so,' I lied. 'Not everyone. But we did get an announcement in Assembly about not talking to strangers.'

She started crying again.

'Phelps didn't mention your name. I promise.' I leant over to hug her but she pulled away.

'Is it my fault?' I asked her. 'I mean were you coming to the pub to meet us when it happened?'

'Don't be stupid, Becs,' she said trying to smile. 'Not everything is your fault.'

'But were you coming?'

'No, Becs. I don't want to talk about it. Please.' She wiped her nose. 'Just do one thing for me, though. Can you just get everyone not to talk about it? I feel so embarrassed.'

'I'll try,' I said. 'I could get Sal to help.'

Mary-Jane's face crumpled again. 'I just don't want anyone to know. Okay, Becs?'

'Okay.'

She rested her chin on her folded knees again and carried on staring into space. I stroked her back in the same way that Mum used to stroke mine when I was sick, gently running my fingers in little circles.

'Please don't,' she mumbled.

So I just sat there in silence beside her.

Her room was like a time warp. Nothing had changed since we were little. There was the out-of-control yucca plant on her windowsill, the photo of us together on our first day of school and her stack of old *Jackie* magazines.

I picked one up. I thought maybe I should read to her to take her mind off it.

'Have you read this one yet?' I asked, flicking through to the problem page.

Mary-Jane ignored my question so I just started reading.

Magazines were banned at home. I was only allowed to read 'literature', i.e. books to prepare me for university. Dad was a serious idiot, though. *Jackie* was the only place we learnt anything about the real world and more importantly sex.

'Listen to this,' I said. 'Dear Cathy and Clare, my best friend has fallen in love with my brother and…'

'Becs. Stop. Just don't.'

'I'm only reading to you.'

'Just don't.'

'Okay,' I said and went back to reading silently. There wasn't anything particularly juicy in it anyway. Not like the time they had a letter from a girl asking what a French kiss was. We'd memorized the answer so we'd know what to do when the time came.

Stuck above Mary-Jane's dressing table with its corners curling up round the edges was the portrait she did of me in the last year of Primary. Underneath in purple felt-tip was written 'My best friend for life'.

We used to be able to talk about everything. After Mum went I used to fall asleep huddled against her for comfort. I wish she'd talk now. I wish she'd say if it was my fault.

I suddenly felt incredibly lonely sitting beside her in her silent room, like the astronaut in 'Space Oddity', suspended in eternity.

I put the copy of *Jackie* down. Mary-Jane just carried on hugging her knees like I didn't exist. Maybe if I told her about Bracken it would take her mind off things. She'd be excited for me. I ought to tell her anyway. Not telling her was a kind of lie, what Dad would've called a crime of omission. He was a barrister and according to him sometimes not doing something could make you guilty of a crime.

But just then Mrs Hamilton came in carrying a tray of tea and scones, her hair plaited and then twisted up around her head with kirby grips.

'Hello, Becs,' she said and put the tray down so she could hug me. 'Thanks for coming over. MJ's had a bit of a fright, poor thing.'

'I know.'

'How about a cuppa?' She was trying to sound breezy and normal but there was nothing normal about the situation. Mary-Jane wasn't moving.

'How's school?' she asked, squishing some jam onto a scone. 'Have you started revising yet?'

'Sort of,' I said. 'What about Mary-Jane? When do you think she'll be coming back?'

Mary-Jane started crying. Her mum mimed a silent shhh to me. I stood at the door for a moment and watched as she went over and pulled Mary-Jane into her arms, cuddling her as she had when she was little. Then I turned and left.

Chapter 5

As we walked into the playground two police officers with flat hats and polished shoes walked out. Sal rushed after them to find out what was going on. They all knew her because of Wayne.

'Someone else got done,' she said, her ponytail swinging and flicks flapping. 'A younger kid this time. Wouldn't say which one. But it wasn't serious. Didn't have to touch it or anything.'

'At least Mary-Jane's not the only one now,' said Pen.

'When's she coming back?' asked Marion.

'She won't be back for ages,' said Sal. 'She doesn't want anyone to see her.'

'Have you seen her?' asked Marion.

'Duh!' said Sal. 'I just said she doesn't want anyone to see her so how could I have seen her?'

'Then how do you know?' persisted Marion.

Sal gave Marion one of her stares. 'It's ob-vi-ous, thicko. How'd you feel if you'd had to touch some old bloke's ding-a-ling and everyone knew about it? Not that any bloke would ever let you near his crown jewels.'

We picked our way through the playground past younger girls playing French elastic and boys trading cigarette cards. I didn't tell them I'd seen Mary-Jane. Sal would've thought I was trying to get one up on her. And anyway, Mary-Jane didn't want everyone gossiping.

Just ahead of us Fenella Jones was dragging her cello into school. Phil and Dom rushed her from behind.

'Morning, Bog Brush,' shouted Phil as Dom smacked her on the bum.

Sal roared with laughter. Bog Brush was the perfect name for her on account of her tight white curly hair.

'Bog Brush, Bog Brush,' chanted Phil and Dom and before long a small crowd had gathered and joined in.

I hung behind and pretended to pull up my white socks. There was nothing I could do to help, Fenella was a sitting duck. Mum had made me go to her house for tea once. Her kitchen was full of dressmakers' dummies and music stands and they didn't have a TV. She should have begged her parents to send her to a different school.

At break I hid in the library and thought about Bracken.

I pulled out the *Penguin Book of Love Poetry* and read e e cummings's 'It may not always be so' followed by Christina Rossetti's 'Remember' to elevate my thinking.

Then I went over every detail of what had happened with Bracken. I needed to try to ration how many times I went over it so I didn't wear it out. I read a story once about how after some nuclear holocaust there was only one record left in the whole world. The man who found it had to decide when and how often to play it. He knew that each time he played it the record would grow thinner and more scratched until eventually it would wear out and there'd be no music left on earth at all.

That's how I felt about Bracken. When I replayed the memory of how he'd held me I still felt a charge of electricity jolt through me but each time it grew slightly weaker. I couldn't bear to think that one day I might not be able to feel it at all.

After school I went to the newsagents to choose a card for Mary-Jane. I picked up a Sherbet Dip Dab for Fenella. I'd sneak it into her pocket so that something nice would've happened to her. If she ever gave me the chance, I'd tell her what she needed to do to fit in but she didn't really talk to anybody any more.

The only card I could find that didn't have 'Happy Birthday' or 'Congratulations on Your Retirement' on it had a cartoon of Charlie Brown saying 'Cheer Up, It May Never Happen'. It would have to do and I passed it round the bus asking everyone to write a message for her.

Sarah Slater asked Les to sign it and we all huddled round to see what he'd written.

'Regards Les,' read Sal. 'Couldn't he even have put a kiss?' She snatched the pencil from Sarah and added two x's after his name.

'It counts as an autograph,' said Marion, examining it.

She was right – Mary-Jane probably would glue it into her small leather autograph book alongside all the show jumpers' ones she'd got at the Horse of the Year Show.

As I got off the bus Dave had snatched Les's copy of the *Sun* and tried to shove it into one of his jacket pockets.

'Go on, Les, you've read it already,' he was saying. 'I'll bring it back tomorrow, promise.'

'No you don't,' said Les. 'It belongs right here beside me and that's where it's staying.' Les grabbed it back and put it on the dashboard next to the tattered photo of a small boy that he kept taped there. Dave stood there like a dog without his bone.

'Why don't you stick to Marx?' I said as I pushed past him.

'Pathetic, isn't it?' said Pete as he slammed the bus door. 'Really pathetic.'

Pete was the only boy who didn't gawp at page 3. He was so much cooler than the others realized.

'Very pathetic,' I said and felt myself blush.

The bus spluttered off. Pete kicked a small stone from one foot to the other and then pulled a battered pack of Marlboros out of his jacket.

'The stuff my dad's got,' he said and for the first time I got to look into his eyes and saw they were deep set and piercing blue. 'Now that's worth getting excited about.'

Pete had never actually spoken to me before. Normally once the bus had gone he'd just wander off through the oak entrance gates that stood on either side of his front drive.

'My dad's got everything,' he continued. 'He gets it imported from Sweden. The real thing. Those twats wouldn't know what hit them if they saw it.' He lit his fag and took a long lazy drag. 'I'll show you some time if you like.'

He puffed out rings as he waited for me to say something

and when I didn't because I was so stunned I didn't know what to say he just shrugged.

'Think about it,' he said as he swung his canvas record bag over his shoulder and sauntered off.

Chapter 6

I'd never thought of Mary-Jane's lane as spooky before. But as soon as I started to wonder about where exactly it had happened to her, the trees that lined it on either side spontaneously transformed themselves into grizzled old men with long lunging arms in place of branches. The bushes that lay beyond, where we'd always looked for blackberries, were the perfect hiding place for a stranger to lurk and then pounce.

I stood up to pedal faster but it was hard to pick up speed – the surface was bumpy with a ridge along the middle where bits of grass poked through. In my basket the book of poems I'd brought to read to Mary-Jane if she was silent again somersaulted up and down, crushing the flowers I'd picked from the garden.

I was going as fast as I could but it still felt dangerously slow. Just then I heard a noise. An engine coming up behind me. I tried to pedal more quickly but I was already at full tilt. It was right behind me now. The lane wasn't wide enough for it to go past. What would happen if it was him – the bloke who'd got Mary-Jane? What would happen if he just ran me down? I forced my bike up onto the grass verge and jumped off. I knew there was a break in the bushes just a little ahead. I ran as fast as I could through the gap and into the field. I didn't stop to prop up my bike, I just let it fall and then ran. I ran across the dry field where wheat was supposed to be growing and through the fallow field beyond and it was only when I got to the Mill Pond that I stopped.

I crouched down and hid in the rushes that surrounded the water. I'd wait, I decided, until everything was quiet and it was safe to come out. I scrunched a dent into the brown reeds and lay down as flat as I could to avoid detection.

A lone mallard paddled across the grey-green water. When Mary-Jane and I were nine or ten we'd gone camping there with her dad and found a nest of fluffy ducklings. In the morning there'd been a terrible squawking sound as a Canada goose, neck curved into an elegant arch, had taken each duckling and held it under the water until it drowned. Mary-Jane shouted at her dad to do something.

'There's nothing to be done,' he'd told her. 'The pond's overpopulated. The goose is just keeping numbers down. It's nature's way.'

Mary-Jane flew at him screaming, fists flying. 'You have to do something. You have to save them.'

And when he told her again there was nothing he could do she plunged into the water to try to stop the goose herself. Of course, she couldn't get to it. The water was too deep, the reeds too thick and her clothes too heavy. Her dad waded in to save her. I can still remember how white her skin looked when he peeled her clothes off and wrapped her in a camping blanket. When we spoke about it afterwards she said it was less what the goose had done that had upset her and more that her dad hadn't been able to do anything to stop it.

A swarm of tiny black flies started to circle me so I decided to risk heading home. It didn't feel safe to go back to the lane so instead I headed straight for the main road.

As I was nearly at the road I heard an engine again. I crouched down but then a familiar whiff of oily smoke made me hesitate. Seconds later the school bus rounded the corner on its way back into town. Les pulled over and leant out the window.

'You all right?'

'Yes,' I said, bursting into tears.

'Hop in. I'll give you a ride.'

'But I've left my bike behind,' I said.

Les sat me down in the front seat and told me to wait there while he went up the lane to find my bike. Sitting alone on the empty bus was weird, like seeing someone's mum without her make-up on.

I took a humbug from the jar and noticed the creased black-and-white photo Les kept on the dashboard. The boy in it had shaggy hair and dark squinty eyes that seemed to go in opposite directions.

'That's Ian,' said Les, carrying my bike on and wedging it between two rows of seats. 'He's about your age now. That was taken years ago.'

'Does he go to our school?' I asked.

Les laughed gently. 'No, love,' he said. 'Ian doesn't go to school. He's crippled. Spastic. Stays at home with my missus.'

'I'm sorry.'

'Don't be. Not your fault. Matter of fact I was just on my way to take them shopping now – but keep that to yourself.' Les tapped a finger to his lips. 'Unofficial perk of the job. This old tank can fit him and his wheelchair in. No problem.'

As he reversed the bus into Mary-Jane's lane to turn around, the low-hanging branches drummed against the roof. Mary-Jane's card was still in my bike basket but the book and the flowers had gone. I imagined them lying dusty somewhere in the dry field and the poems disintegrating the next time it rained, that is if it ever did rain again. According to Dad it was the driest spring since the reign of George II.

Les leant across, his belly hanging over his trousers, and pushed in a tape.

It's now or never, sang Elvis.

'You listen to the King,' Les said. 'He knows what's what. Anyway, you shouldn't be out on your own. Not while there's a nutter on the loose.'

Chapter 7

He was waiting on the pavement outside school.

I didn't actually see him until he was standing right in front of me, blocking my path.

'Watcha,' Bracken said. 'Took me a while to find you. I didn't know what school you were at.'

I didn't say anything. I just stood there stunned. He grinned. The same lopsided grin I'd been dreaming about.

'Hop in then,' he said, tilting his head towards his van, which I now saw was parked right behind him on the double yellow lines. Nobody ever parked there, smack bang outside school. 'Had to park where I could be sure I'd see you,' he said, grinning again. 'This was the last school on my list. I'd nearly given up hope.'

He held the passenger door open for me. I tried to act as if this was all normal. Like I was perfectly used to finding hunky handsome men waiting for me at the school gates. I climbed in, feeling like it was all happening to someone else. I was aware of the people walking past us on the pavement;

my foot on the white metal step; Bracken's arm helping me up; the black plastic seat burning hot against the back of my legs as I sat down; my legs shaking; my heart hammering. But it felt like a film, real and not real at the same time and certainly not happening to me. There was a clunk as Bracken slammed the door shut and then before I knew it he was there beside me in the driver's seat, revving the engine and ramming it into gear. The tyres squealed as we sped off. I couldn't help hoping people had seen.

He turned left at the end of the road. I saw the school bus parked with the others all lined up waiting to climb into it. As we sailed past I wondered if they'd notice that I wasn't there, and what they'd think.

Bracken pushed a tape into the machine. Bob Dylan. 'Blowin' in the Wind'.

'I love this one,' I said, but my voice sounded thin, shy. Scared.

'I thought you would.'

Some of the cherry trees that lined the road by the park were already starting to bloom; there were crimson blossoms in the tub outside the petrol station. There seemed to be flowers everywhere. I hadn't noticed them before.

'So, how was your day?' Bracken asked. Like it was completely normal that he'd picked me up. Like it was what happened every day and we were just continuing a conversation we'd started that morning over breakfast.

I tried to sound casual. 'It was fine. How about yours?'

'It just got a whole load better.' His top lip curled into its crooked smile. He was like Heathcliff and Mr Rochester rolled into one.

He ran a hand through his messy black hair and cleared his throat a bit like Dad did sometimes when he was about to say something important.

'You know what, Red?' he said quietly.

'Red?'

'Red,' he replied, like it was settled that that was now my name.

'What?' I asked, leaning across to hear him.

'This might sound daft,' his voice got even softer and he reached a hand out to hold mine, 'but I've really missed you. There's just something about you. I dunno. Something. Just haven't been able to get you out of my head.'

You have no idea, I thought, feeling as if my heart was about to soar out of my body, crash through the roof of the van and start orbiting the earth. I felt myself blush.

For some reason an image of Mary-Jane sitting on her bed flashed into my mind. Maybe I felt guilty because I was there falling in love while she was all upset and alone in her room. It was the opposite of how it'd been all our lives. Usually it was the good things that happened to her.

We sped through the centre of town, past the cinema and the entrance to the park. As we passed the public library I told him about how I hung out there when I was feeling sad and lonely and missing Mum.

'You won't need to do that any more,' he said. He kept one hand resting on the gear stick and drove fast, like he knew what he was doing. While he was staring at the road I could sneak glances and take in his profile. His nose was long with a small kink halfway down: manly, not a boyish snub. I liked that it was real rather than perfect. Underneath a thick layer of stubble, a small dimple appeared when he smiled.

I can't properly explain how handsome he was. But it was like David Essex or Robert Redford had stepped out of a poster and sat down next to me, which was magical but also scary.

Quite soon we were on Station Road and then before I knew it we'd pulled up outside Mick's Chip Shop.

'Does anyone still come here?' he asked, cracking his knuckles. 'We always did after school.'

'Yes,' I said, although I wasn't allowed to go myself – according to Dad, it was a dump and not the sort of place his daughter should ever be seen at.

He bought me chips and added salt and vinegar without asking, a can of R Whites too. There was a group of boys from my year in the corner fishing in their pockets to get enough change together to buy a bag of chips.

'Get her,' I heard one of them say as we walked out. I could feel them all staring as I got back in the van and, for a second, I didn't feel shy. I felt proud. Proud I was not with some stupid schoolboy but with someone who could drive and had a job and understood how the world worked.

We started driving again. I still didn't know where we were going. Every so often Bracken reached over and helped himself to a chip out of the pile on my lap. It just felt right, as if we'd always been doing things like drive in his van together sharing chips.

'What time do you have to be home?' he asked. 'I don't want you to be late.'

'Not for a while,' I said. 'Dad's never back from work before seven when he's got a case on.'

'Good,' Bracken said. He pulled some shades out of his jacket pocket and put them on so now he looked like James Dean. We carried on up Station Road, over the iron bridge and round behind the station past The Wheatsheaf where the bad boys went to get pissed. We drove on for a few minutes more before turning left into the industrial estate. I'd never been down there before, I never even knew it existed. We passed rows of smart, low-rise brick and glass buildings and then on to a smaller road, where bulldozers and diggers had been at work. It twisted and turned until finally we couldn't go any further. It was a dead end. Bracken stopped the van and turned off the engine.

'Here we are,' he said. 'Not much but it's all mine.'

He pointed over to a small building with a corrugated iron roof. It was no bigger than the double garage we had at home for Dad's car. It was just standing there alone, on a big patch of concrete with a battered Reliant Robin parked outside. It wasn't like the modern buildings we'd been driving past, it looked left behind, forgotten. The Robin had a dent on the front and was missing a wheel. Above the building a sign said 'S. Bracken Autos' in thick black painted letters, the same as it said on his van.

Bracken jumped out and before I'd had time to bundle up the chip paper he was round to my side, opening the door.

'Allow me,' he said and offered his hand.

I followed him across the cracked concrete. Weeds crept out of the gaps, their leaves bright against the drab grey.

'Duh-da,' he said, lifting up the garage door. A large bee

flew out of the darkness and, blinded by the light, crashed into me. I jumped back. Suddenly scared. Maybe I should leave, run back across the concrete and somehow find my way home.

But then Bracken was saying, 'Let's do this right,' and the next thing I knew he'd scooped me up into his arms and was carrying me across the threshold like I was his bride and I was back in the fairytale.

Inside it was soot black. The air was dense with dust and the smell of petrol. Bracken put me down and pulled a cord. A naked bulb flickered into life. As my eyes adjusted I could make out a stack of metal shelves on the back wall with bits of engines and tools on it.

Parked in the middle was a yellow car with the bonnet propped open. Everything felt greasy. I was confused. I thought there'd be petrol pumps or other people in overalls working or racks of tyres or a cash register.

'Is this it?' I asked, realizing too late that I sounded rude.

''Fraid so.' Bracken's face clouded over. He picked up a spanner and I noticed the tip of his little finger was missing. There was an uncomfortable silence while he fiddled with something under the bonnet. When he turned back to me he was smiling again, calm. He put the spanner down, wiped his hands on his jeans, cracked his knuckles and came over to me.

Slowly and deliberately, he took the lemonade can out of my hand and put it on the shelves. He paused for a moment, then stepped forward and took hold of me like he did in the pub. Firmly. Like I had no choice. Like I belonged to him.

A tiny voice inside my head was wondering whether I

should be there with this man, wherever 'there' was. Another part of me was worrying about whether my uniform looked stupid; whether it mattered that I hadn't got any eye shadow on or checked my breath. Then Bracken tilted his head down and kissed me and I forgot it all. I forgot about my outfit and about school and about the small dark building we were standing in. I forgot that maybe I ought to be scared, I forgot about everything except for him and me.

He put one arm around my shoulders, pulling me tightly to him. With the other hand he grabbed the back of my grey school skirt and yanked me closer to him. When I was as close to him as I could possibly be he started pushing himself against me. It felt good, like it did when we were dancing. Like we were governed by a feeling bigger and more powerful and more profound than either of us could control.

He kissed me deeper and deeper. I was no longer scared that I wasn't doing it right. This couldn't be anything but right. I waited for him to go further, to lift my skirt or to slide his hand up under my white nylon shirt. But he didn't. We just kissed for ages, our bodies locked together, his tongue searching out mine, his lips moving and sucking and pulling.

Eventually he paused, buried his head in my hair, and breathed in.

My heart was hammering. I'd never let anyone do anything other than kiss me before, not touch me or feel me, but with Bracken I felt ready. I felt ready for anything.

'I want to do so much more,' he whispered, like he could hear my thoughts. But he didn't move. He didn't take it further. He just held me, his head buried in my hair.

'Red,' he whispered. 'My Red.'

And then he was silent and we stood there entwined and motionless, holding each other as if time had stopped.

By the time he dropped me at the end of my lane it was late, after eight. I should've felt worried about Dad; he was going to go ballistic. I should've worried about my English essay, which was due in tomorrow. We were meant to write about the role of fate in *Tess of the D'Urbervilles* because it was bound to come up in the exams. But I hadn't started it and I couldn't be bothered to think about it now. I felt untouchable, soaring, free, weightless.

Chapter 8

The next morning Sal was acting odd. She sat next to Pen whispering so I couldn't hear a word of what she was saying. It was the first time since she'd decided we were best friends that she didn't just plonk herself down next to me. I watched her black glossy ponytail swish from side to side as she laughed loudly at everything Pen said.

I'd always longed for shiny hair like hers. Mum used to say the secret was to brush your hair a hundred times each night. I'd always refused to but when Mum went I started brushing it like mad, hoping that, like Aladdin rubbing his magic lamp, brushing my hair might make a genie appear and bring Mum back.

At school, everyone was talking about some girl in the second form who was sure she'd seen the bloke near the station. She'd dialled 999 from a payphone but the operator hadn't believed her.

In the loos at break-time Sal finally spoke to me.

'So who was that then? School bus not good enough for you any more?'

'Just a friend.'

Sal went over to the mirror and started squeezing a black-head on her chin. I stood there, mute, staring at her ponytail, waiting for her to ask me more. When she didn't, I bent down and pretended to adjust my socks. Then I took my hair out of its elastic and retied it, waiting for Sal to speak.

She finished with her chin and checked her profile, then she picked up her books.

'A bit of a cradle-snatcher, isn't he?' she said as she reached the door. 'Gave me the creeps.'

I couldn't let her see me cry so I darted into one of the cubicles and rattled the loo roll holder so it'd sound like I was having a pee. The door slammed as Sal left and then the bell went.

'She's just jealous,' a voice said. I came out of the loo and saw Marion there. 'He wasn't creepy, he was dead gorgeous. Where'd you find someone like him?'

'The pub,' I said and Marion giggled.

'Has he got any mates?' she asked as we headed off to Maths.

I couldn't concentrate in Maths. I couldn't concentrate in any of the lessons. It was partly thinking about Bracken and partly everybody talking about the flasher and who was going to be next.

At lunchtime the police were back. Sal rolled her skirt up to turn it into a mini and rushed across to chat to them. One of them was Wayne's mate so she gave him a hug, which made

47

Phelps go crazy, shouting at her to show some decorum. He made her unfurl her skirt and threatened her with a detention. As soon as he'd gone inside with the coppers she rolled it back up again and redid her tie so it was short and stubby the same as boys always wore theirs.

In Biology it was my turn to get into trouble. I was meant to be drawing a diagram of a hydra but instead I doodled a 3D heart with Bracken's name inside. Unfortunately, Mrs O'Dwyer caught me. I managed to scribble over it so she couldn't see Bracken's name but she gave me a detention anyway. It was the first I'd ever had. I was meant to be Mrs OD's star pupil, get all A's and become a doctor so that she wouldn't feel her life in the classroom had been wasted.

Usually I'd have been really upset and scared of what Dad would say but today I couldn't care less. Education in general and O levels in particular were starting to feel really irrelevant. Poxy, as Sal would've said.

When school was finally over, I didn't dare look to see if Bracken was there. He hadn't said he would come. He hadn't said anything about when I'd see him next. I slid my hair free from its elastic, shook it loose and tried to rake it straight with my fingers. Just in case. I walked slowly across the playground with Marion, pretending to concentrate on what she was saying although I actually had no idea what she was on about. Sal appeared from nowhere chewing gum and walking with the wiggle she'd designed to look sexy to anyone who was behind her. She was all outraged that she wasn't allowed to hug Wayne's friend and she put her arm through Marion's, pulling her close even though she never usually bothered with her.

'Come on, M, let's not miss the bus. Becs has got her love machine to go to.'

I looked up. Bracken was standing beside his van in his sunglasses smiling and holding open the passenger door.

'Watcha,' he said.

'Watcha,' I replied, blushing.

A can of Tizer and a tube of Spangles were waiting for me on the passenger seat when I climbed in.

'Thought you might want a snack,' he said and put his foot down so the tyres squealed again as we drove off.

The windows were open and a warm breeze blew between us whipping my hair as we sped through the town centre listening to the Eagles.

'Good day?' he asked.

I nodded, crunching on a Spangle. And then because I felt awkward and shy and couldn't think of what to say, I reached across and stroked his leg. He put his hand on mine and squeezed it.

We drove out of town a different way today. Bracken wouldn't say where we were going but eventually, when we reached the scrubland by the reservoir, he pulled over into a lay-by. We kissed until our lips were sore and then he led me by the hand across the dry mud to the water tower, which squatted like a giant concrete rocket next to the treatment plant. It looked cool like it belonged on the cover of a Pink Floyd LP.

Without a word Bracken started climbing the metal ladder that ran up its outside and nodded to me to follow.

Our feet clanked on the rungs. Above us the sky was a cloud-less blue. I wondered if this was how Neil Armstrong had felt climbing into Apollo 11. Terrified and excited. When I paused to look down I felt dizzy. The reservoir looked small and had brown rings round it where the water level had sunk like a huge dirty concrete bath. When I tried again to ask Bracken what we were doing here he put a finger to his lips to tell me to be quiet.

Halfway up he stopped climbing and pointed to a ledge. A large bird with long black tail feathers sat on a nest of broken bricks and loose cement. A moment later it took flight, yellow feet dangling, slate-grey wings extended.

'Take a look quick.' Bracken pulled me up closer to him. 'Before she comes back.'

There, nestled in the dent of the Spartan nest, sat three downy chicks.

'Falcons,' Bracken said proudly like he'd hatched them himself. He took a plastic bag from his pocket and carefully tipped something stinky and pink onto the ledge. 'Mince,' he explained. 'They love it. Took it off Mum's dogs. Now, quick scarper before she comes back.'

When we were back on the ground she swooped down towards us close enough so I could see the glint of her eye and the point of her beak. Then she soared up to the nest, her speckled breast a flash across the spotless blue sky.

'She could have attacked us,' I said.

'Not her,' said Bracken. 'Been doing this ever since she lost her fella. Some poser in a Jag hit him, didn't even stop. She stood there by his body shrieking and clicking like that would bring him back to life. Horrible, heartbroken noise it was. Then she flew back up here. Was worried they wouldn't survive without their breadwinner, so I've been up every day. They mate for life, you know.'

Dad was standing in the hall as I let myself in. He was home early, which usually meant something had gone wrong in court. He'd managed to find a way of being paid for being pompous, standing up pontificating in court so that the 'wrong kind of people' were put behind bars. Pen's little brother Dave said barristers like Dad helped prop up the cap-italist regime. He said Dad would be first against the wall when the communists took over.

'What sort of time do you call this, young lady, why weren't you on the bus?' His collarless shirt flapped open revealing how his neck sagged like a turkey's.

I didn't answer.

'Where have you been?' The door to his study was open. A huge mound of papers with pink ribbons round them sat on his desk.

'Nowhere,' I said, and then added, 'I was doing revision and missed the bus and didn't have any money so I had to walk home.'

'Are you mentally subnormal?' He always sounded like he was in court. 'You walked three and a half miles home when there's a predator on the loose?'

'No lions and tigers in Essex,' I muttered. As usual his breath stank.

'Have you any idea what could have happened to you?' He raised his voice. 'Rebecca. I will not have my daughter wandering around the countryside when there's a criminal at large. Do you understand?'

I gauged the distance between him and the wall. Just enough room to slip past.

'How about being pleased,' I shouted back as I ran up the stairs, 'pleased that I've actually been doing some revision like you always want me to.'

I examined my face in the oval mirror above my chest of drawers. Even though I'd given up believing in God at much the same time as I'd discovered Father Christmas was a lie, I couldn't help feeling like I'd sinned.

I thought about Hester Prynne, in *The Scarlet Letter*, and the 'A' she was forced to wear on her clothes so that everyone knew she was an adulteress. I couldn't help worrying there might be a visible mark of shame on me. But there was nothing other than a top lip that was ever so slightly swollen from so much kissing.

Normally homework distracted me, but I couldn't concentrate. It wasn't just Bracken, it was Dad. Whenever Dad got angry I felt guilty. He was useless without Mum. I don't remember him ever getting drunk before she left. It was stupid that we both sat in our separate rooms missing her. There were so many things I longed to ask him about her like which was her favourite Quality Street and whether she'd had freckles when she was little like me. But I was banned from even mentioning her. Dad had decreed that she didn't exist any more.

I tiptoed downstairs. Dad was bent over a pile of papers, his shiny bald head reflecting the lights of the chandelier above. Behind him were the glass cabinets where he kept his collection of dead butterflies. Mum used to call the study his mausoleum. He had his whisky decanter beside him. For a moment he didn't look powerful and evil at all – he looked more like the lonely old man who'd pretended to be the Wizard of Oz in the film. I could feel the weight of his sadness as if it was my own.

'Are you ready to go through for dinner?' I asked.

Dad looked up from his work, irritated.

It was my job to bring the food through from the kitchen. Dad didn't have time to cook so he paid Mrs Turner to make something while she was here cleaning. I used the pot holder to take out the two plates she'd left in the Aga. Veal escalopes, pureed potato and peas, or 'petits pois' as Dad insisted we called them. The 'petits pois' looked tiny and shrivelled, like fingertips after a long bath.

I carried the plates into the dining room. Our places were laid out as usual, opposite each other at the mahogany dining table. There was always a bottle of red wine at Dad's end. I used to time how long he took to drink it. His record was six minutes.

I had to wait for Dad to unfold his napkin before I was allowed to start eating. That was one of the rules. Another was that I wasn't to speak unless spoken to because Dad might be thinking. When he was in a good mood and he didn't need to think about something he'd start a conversation on a topic he found interesting like Ancient Greece or how a hosepipe ban would destroy England's lawns. Sometimes he tried to explain a legal principle like the presumption of innocence, or worse still he talked about his latest specimen of butterfly. But mostly, like tonight, we sat in silence.

After dinner I cleared the table and stacked the plates for when Mrs Turner came back in the morning. Then Dad let me watch *Tomorrow's World* because he considered it to be educational. What I really wanted to watch was *Top of the Pops* or *Jim'll Fix It*, like everyone else, but he never allowed that.

There was an item about how one day cars would be able to run on batteries rather than petrol and Dad got all excited about how then we'd have the Arabs on the run.

By the time the nine o'clock news had come on Dad had fallen fast asleep and was snoring, mouth open. The newscaster was going on about Harold Wilson's resignation. I crept up to the TV to see if I could switch it to something more interesting.

'We need to talk, young lady.' Dad was awake. His face was dimpled down one side with the imprint of the armchair.

'What about?' I tried to sound nonchalant.

'How you're spending your time.' His eyes closed again. 'I want an accounting...'

He suspects, I thought, as he fell back asleep.

The French doors were open. I walked out into the garden and followed the narrow stone path down to the end of the lawn where the apple tree stood, its branches a delicate filigree silhouetted against the night sky. Mum had always wanted to plant an orchard around it. But it had remained a solitary fruit tree, a monument to what might have been.

I pressed my cheek against the gnarled bark and tried to remember the sound of Mum's voice. I've met someone, I whispered to her.

Chapter 9

Assembly. We stood shoulder to shoulder. Jam-packed. Bored. Someone in the back row, probably Dom, let rip and so we all covered our mouths, mock coughing and spluttering. Phelps glared in our direction and everyone reluctantly shut up.

Some visiting expert was droning on about personal safety. Kindergarten stuff. Don't accept lifts from strangers, scream if you're attacked, etc. If someone's following you, ask a grown-up for help, preferably a woman with children. I wanted to put my hand up and ask how many women with kids he thought were wandering the lanes where Mary-Jane and I lived. But I didn't. I never actually dared cause trouble at school.

On the wall beside me hung the wooden plaque engraved with the names of all the ex-pupils who'd died fighting in the Second World War.

I stared at the rows of heads in front of me. Hundreds of them. Some neat, some scruffy. If we'd been born forty years earlier, all the boys would soon have been sent off to war and died, and all the girls would've been left behind with nobody to marry. Why did I get to be born now and not then? Maybe it was so I could meet Bracken.

Suddenly, Marion dug me in the elbow and whispered, 'What've you been up to?'

'What?' I whispered back.

'You're on the list. Phelps just said your name.'

'You're taking the piss?'

Marion shook her head.

All morning I got more and more anxious. By lunchtime, when I went to wait outside Phelps's office, I thought I might actually throw up. Anything could happen. Letter home. Expulsion. Police. Phelps's secretary was clattering away on her typewriter. She didn't meet my eye when I tried to smile at her. As I stood in the line I thought about how many times I'd swanned past the kids waiting there and thought what idiots they were. Now I was one of them and there was only one conceivable reason why I was here: Bracken. There wasn't anything else. The vice on my stomach tightened another notch. Maybe a teacher had seen me in his van. Maybe one of my friends had grassed me up. But what were they going to do me for? Riding in a van? Having a boyfriend? None of that was a crime. It wasn't like he was coming into school or disrupting lessons or anything.

A year ago I'd been in the Headmaster's office to collect a certificate for coming top in the end-of-year exams. The school had the 'highest hopes' for me, he'd beamed, which Dad said meant Oxford or Cambridge.

Today Phelps sat at his desk writing something in a large hardback ledger as if I didn't exist. There was no chair for me to sit on. Through the window above his head I watched a plane leave a vapour trail as it carved its way across the clear sky. After what seemed like an eternity he clicked the lid back onto his fountain pen and looked up.

'I'm disappointed to see you here, Rebecca,' he said, rolling the pen between his fingers like Dad rubbed his cigars. 'Not what I expect from a girl like you.'

'Sorry, Sir.'

I still didn't know what it was I was meant to be remorseful for.

'I expect better from you. I expect you to set an example, a good one.'

'Yes, Sir.'

'Missing a detention is serious. It'll go on your record. Could well damage your chances of becoming a prefect. If it wasn't for your past good conduct, you'd be getting a letter home.'

The detention that Mrs O'Dwyer gave me. Of course! I was so relieved it wasn't anything to do with Bracken that I almost laughed out loud.

'Would you like to enlighten me as to the source of your amusement?'

'Sorry, Sir,' I said. 'I don't know what happened, I completely forgot I had it.'

Outside in the playground people kept coming up to me to find out what had gone on with Phelps.

'I told him he and Mrs OD could stuff his poxy detention,' I said.

Dom slapped me on the back.

'Right on,' Sarah Slater said, giving me the peace sign. 'They shouldn't be giving them out in the first place. It's all wrong.'

I let everyone think I didn't care, and with each person I told I felt stronger, cooler. It was liberating. It felt like I was cracking out of a shell that had become too small. A new me was emerging. One that didn't have to be so scared or so good.

I raced out of school to see if Bracken was there, but just as I got to the gate, someone grabbed my arm.

'Not so fast, Rebecca,' said Mrs OD. 'You can't have forgotten your detention again?'

'I can't. I'm sorry. Can I do it tomorrow?' There were too many people piling out of the gate for me to see whether Bracken was waiting there or not.

'Absolutely not.'

'I've got a doctor's appointment, can I do it tomorrow instead, I'll do double?'

'We had better call your father, if that's the case.' She took my arm and started to steer me in the direction of the school office.

'No, don't do that,' I fumbled. 'He's got a big case on. He hates to be disturbed. I can go to the doctor's tomorrow.'

'Your poor father does have enough on his plate,' Mrs OD agreed, 'so we won't call him this time. But next time I won't hesitate. You've hardly been set the best example by your mother.'

I stuck two fingers up at Mrs OD's back and followed her to the lab where she made me scrub the benches. I worked extra fast hoping Bracken would still be there if she let me out early for good behaviour.

In between a group of Petri dishes, I found a small tubular squishy stump that looked alarmingly like part of a worm. I'd refused to do dissection on moral grounds. Just because worms aren't cute doesn't mean they can't feel. I wrapped the stump in a tissue and said a quick prayer as I buried it in the bin.

When I'd finished I asked if I could be excused; if I was lucky, Bracken wouldn't have gone. But Mrs OD shook her head and pointed to a metal bucket and string cloth and told me to scrub the floor.

From my position on all fours, her bun resembled a lump growing out of the back of her head. I knew why she was making a meal out of it. She liked Dad. She lived opposite the greengrocer's and was always bumping into him accidentally on purpose. We called her Mrs even though she was a spinster because she was too old to be a Miss.

'Miss, have you ever reproduced?' Dom had asked her once.

'Sex outside of marriage is a sin,' she'd replied, patting her bun.

'Miss, Miss, I'll marry you,' the boys started up.

'More like she couldn't get anyone to go near her,' Sal had whispered and we'd all giggled.

When I finally emerged, my eyes stung in the sunlight, like a prisoner being released from a cell. Untucking my shirt I noticed a small hole on the front of it. Singed black round the edge, it must have been a drop of acid. It made me think of the scarlet 'A' pinned to Hester Prynne's chest again. I was so busy examining the mark that I didn't see Bracken until I was outside the school gate.

'You're still here. I can't believe it.'

'Of course, why wouldn't I be?' He reached out and took my bag.

'But I'm so late…'

Maybe Sal or Pen or Marion had told him – I hoped so. Then they'd get why I liked him so much.

'I'll always be here for you,' he said, opening the door of the van so I could climb in and handing me a Flake. 'You're not getting rid of me that easily.'

I opened the crinkly wrapper and slipped my sandals off.

'Red, you do know you're the prettiest of the lot of them, don't you?'

'What?'

'I watch them all come out every day. You're the best by far.'

I blushed and wanted to say that he'd never think that if he'd met Mary-Jane, but instead I pretended to concentrate on scooping up crumbs of chocolate from my skirt.

He reached across and took my hand. 'I just hope you don't wake up one day and say you're too good for me.'

I looked down at our hands, his big fingers gently enfolding mine. 'I wouldn't ever. Not in a million years.'

'Not being funny or anything,' he leant across and with his other hand, the one that only had half a little finger, he pushed a strand of hair from my forehead, 'but I think it's time to take things to the next stage.'

I must have looked scared because then he said, 'Don't worry. We'll go out to dinner first, do things properly.'

I nodded and tried to smile but really I was terrified. Part of me wanted to say I wasn't ready and couldn't we just leave things as they were but another part of me wanted to do everything he wanted me to do so that I didn't disappoint him.

Chapter 10

It was another week before Mary-Jane made it back to school. I hadn't been to visit her. I hadn't had time because of having to see Bracken most days. But I had thought about her. She was there in my mind whenever I was alone, like the base note in a chord tugging at my conscience. I was a rubbish best friend. All thought and no action, as bad as Hamlet.

Nobody else had seen her either. The only person with any news about her was Sarah Slater. Sarah had taken to sitting beside Les at the front of the bus on account of her massive crush, but last Monday she'd darted back to crouch in the aisle beside us.

'Mary-Jane's stopped eating. Our Debbie saw her mum in the Spar, said she won't even eat chocolate.'

'I wish I could stop eating.' Marion fingered the bulge above her waistband.

'Me too,' said Sarah, lifting her shirt up so that we could all see she wasn't fat at all.

'You'd lose your boobs if you got any skinnier,' said Sal.

'Mum used to be a double D, but since her diet my old man said she looks like a dog that's had too many litters.'

Sarah tucked her shirt back in, making sure it was tight across her tits.

'You could be a model,' said Marion. 'Really. She could, couldn't she?'

'Hey Les, do ya think Sarah'd be a good model?' yelled Sal.

'A topless one,' shouted Dom making all the boys hoot with laughter.

Les didn't reply, or look round.

'Yeah, Les, why do you need the *Sun* when you've got Sarah right here?' shouted Pen.

Sarah sashayed up the aisle like it was a catwalk and the boys started wolf-whistling.

'Get 'em off,' shouted Dom.

Sarah laughed and puffed her chest out a little bit more.

The morning that Mary-Jane came back no one laughed. We'd got so used to the bus sailing past her stop that when it pulled over at the end of her lane we were all surprised. We crowded over to the right-hand side to look out of the windows.

She was there. So was her mum, who was holding her arm, which was odd as nobody ever allowed their parents anywhere near the bus stop. Weirder still was that Mary-Jane was wearing her navy winter coat even though it wasn't cold. When the bus door cranked open, her mum shunted her forward, like she was a reluctant carriage on a siding.

Mary-Jane climbed the steps slowly. The skin under her eyes had gone red and flaky. At the top she hesitated, gazing at us all with big wounded eyes like Bambi after his mum had been shot.

We stared back. It was impossible not to. Then someone, I don't know who, started clapping and soon we were all clapping and cheering and shouting 'welcome back' and trying extra hard to make it seem like everything was fine and normal when it clearly was not. Les offered her a humbug and I rushed up to hug her.

'You're so brave,' said Marion once I'd got her sitting down squashed in between us.

'Not really,' said Mary-Jane. 'I didn't have a choice. They said I had to come back or I'd be expelled.' Her hair was tied back in a rubber band. Normally she wouldn't ever do anything that would risk getting split ends. Beneath her coat she was wearing a long-sleeved school shirt. She kept tugging at the cuffs to make them cover her wrists.

Even Dom was freaked out. 'Don't worry, MJ,' he said, stopping by our seat. 'We'll protect you. Phil and I can walk you home if you like.'

Sal was sitting across the aisle and I could see her blush as she fished around in her bag, pretending she wasn't listening to the conversation. Poor Sal, she'd have given anything to have Dom act all chivalrous like that with her.

That afternoon Dom and Phil announced they were on 'perv patrol'. Dom, his sleeves rolled short, paraded up and down the aisle showing off his muscles. Phil took his shirt off completely and rotated on the spot puffing his chest out like he was in the line-up for Mr Universe.

'We're your bodyguards now,' said Phil.

'Yeah, you've got nothing to fear while we're here,' said Dom, laughing at his own rhyme. He really could be a prat.

At Mary-Jane's stop, before she could object, they each took one of her arms and made a big show of escorting her off. Dom took her bag and slung it over his shoulder. We leant against the window as they led her up her lane. Mary-Jane's spindly legs were in thick woolly tights and she looked even narrower with a boy on either side of her.

'Aren't they amazing?' said Marion.

'Real gents,' said Pen.

Sal was the only one of us who hadn't got her face pressed up against the glass. 'If you ask me,' she said, 'she's really milking it.'

'What do you mean?' asked Marion.

'She's not making it up,' said Pen.

'I didn't say she was making it up,' snapped Sal, 'just that she's milking it. Making the most of it, wasn't she, Becs?'

It was the first time Sal had spoken straight to me since my thing with Bracken started. It was an invitation. An offer clear and simple to be friends again. I couldn't resist.

'Looks like it,' I said.

Chapter 11

'Was she all right?' Pete asked as we got off the bus. 'Your friend?'

'I guess so,' I said. Though it was pretty obvious she wasn't.

'Good.' He pulled his fags out and lit one, tilting the packet towards me. I shook my head and then thought maybe I should have taken one, only I didn't smoke. I couldn't. Dad would smell it a mile off and if he didn't kill me he'd have had me locked away in that poncy convent school I nearly went to. I smiled, hoping Pete wouldn't think I was being rude.

'By the way,' he said, 'I've got them.'

'Uh?'

'The mags. You know, my dad's Swedish ones.' He paused, waiting for me to catch on. 'We could look at them some time if you want. You know, you could come over to my place.' His eyes were even bluer than I remembered.

'Isn't it a bit…'

'It's not boring. Those idiots on the bus have got no idea.'

I looked down and realized I was wearing the wrong shoes,

canvas wedges the same as Sal's. One of the webbing straps had started to fray. They suddenly looked cheap.

'It's not that. I mean…' but I couldn't say what I meant, which was that it was weird and even more weird after what had happened to Mary-Jane. So instead I just kept quiet and looked down.

'Your loss,' said Pete, throwing his fag butt onto the ground and walking off without putting it out.

The next day on the bus Pete didn't sit in his normal row just in front of me and the other girls. Instead he swaggered past us down to the back to where Phil was.

Pretty soon we heard Phil shout, 'Unbelievable.'

Then other boys yelled things like 'cor' and 'gedda loada that' extra loudly so everyone would hear.

Dom got on and started hassling Les to let him look at the *Sun* as usual.

'Don't waste your time with that, come and see what Pete's got,' Phil yelled like Pete was just a part of their gang now.

Dom wasn't going to rush for anyone and to prove it he stopped by Fenella Jones who as ever was sitting next to some giant musical instrument to try to hide the fact that she didn't have any friends.

'Morning, Bog Brush,' said Dom in a pretending-to-be-polite voice. 'Oh dear, what's that you've got on your face? Looks like a bug.'

He meant her mole. Poor Fenella. It was large and hairy and sat on the side of her face like a beetle.

'Don't worry, I'll save you, I'll kill it.'

He leant over her. We couldn't see; but we heard the slap, crisp and clear. 'That's it! Got it!'

'Get off!' Fenella let out a glass-shattering scream like the boring guy told us to do in Assembly if anyone tried to interfere with us.

'Dom, stop it. Dom!' Sal yelled, rushing towards the front of the bus to where Fenella was now sobbing.

Dom sauntered nonchalantly to the back, and when they met he pushed past Sal like she was nothing. Sal turned and stuck two fingers up at his back.

'He's a pig,' she said as she sat down next to Fenella. 'A sodding pig,' she repeated more loudly.

The bus stopped suddenly, throwing us all forward.

'What's going on?' asked Les.

'It's Dom's fault,' Sal pronounced. 'He hit her in the face and now she's hysterical.'

Les squeezed past Sal into the seat next to Fenella.

'He's got his arm round her,' Marion, who was standing on her seat to get a better view, reported.

A couple of the younger girls started giggling.

'Yer luck's in there, Fenella,' shouted Pen's little brother Dave. 'Scored at last.'

Eventually, when Fenella's sobs had faded into sniffles, Les strode to the back of the bus. We were all standing on our seats by then to get a better view but he didn't bother to tell us to get down.

'You. You, off,' Les spat, pointing at Dom.

Dom didn't move. He put his arms behind his head like he was making himself comfortable.

'Off,' said Les again and took a step closer.

Dom stared straight back at him. 'Oh yeah, you gonna make me?' Phil shifted over so that he was right beside Dom and also put his hands behind his head so now there were two of them staring Les out.

Les took another step forward and before we knew it he'd grabbed Dom by the collar and lifted him up so they were face-to-face. 'Listen, son,' he said. 'You apologize to that girl or this bus ain't going nowhere.'

It was more dramatic than anything on TV. It looked like Les was going to hit Dom or head-butt him or something.

'Hey Les, old chap.' Pete was on his feet now and taller than Les by a good couple of inches. 'Calm down. Just keep your hair on.'

Les threw Dom back against the seat and turned to Pete, saying, 'This has got fuck all to do with you.'

Turning back to Dom, Les stabbed a finger at his face. 'Listen, son, if you ever, ever do anything to any of the girls on my bus again, you're dead meat.'

He stormed back to the front without looking at any of us. His grey hair, which was normally slicked back Teddy-boy style, hung loose around his face. He tried to push it into place but it kept flopping back.

'Nice one, Dom,' boomed Pete as the bus spluttered into life.

'Nice one, Pete,' said Dom.

'Dead meat, dead meat, dead meat,' chanted a couple of the younger boys.

'One nil to us,' said Phil.

Chapter 12

'I'd like a word with you,' Mrs Jones said to Les. She was wearing a full-length floral dress that hung in a conical shape around her, making it look like she was wearing a wigwam.

Through the window we watched Mrs Jones lecture poor Les, wagging her finger at him as Fenella stared at the ground. Sarah Slater leant over the railing at the front so she could report what was going on.

'She said if Dom wasn't banned from the bus she'd get Les fired.'

'Who the eff does she think she is?' said Sal.

'Said she doesn't want Les putting his arm round her daughter,' continued Sarah.

'He was comforting her. What's wrong with that woman?' said Pen.

'He gave his word that nothing would happen to Fenella again,' continued Sarah. 'Said he'd guarantee her safety personally.'

'She's a pathetic little cry baby. Who tells their mum stuff like that anyway?' said Sal.

'A grass,' I said.

'Grass.' Sal repeated it so that the end of the word hissed like a snake and soon everyone on the bus joined in – 'grass, grass' – to the back of Fenella Jones's head and I wished I'd never said it. It was like I'd given the others a blade to stab her with.

Mary-Jane was the only one who kept quiet. I slipped over to the seat next to her and squeezed her arm but she didn't look at me.

After school, all the girls decided to head to the park to sun-bathe in the unexpectedly warm spring sunshine. Mary-Jane said she had to go home, which we all knew was an excuse. She hadn't taken her coat off once since she came back to school.

'Bring lover boy,' said Sal.

'Yeah, go on,' said Marion. 'I wanna butcher's at him.'

'All right,' I said, wondering if they meant it. 'But don't flirt with him.'

'Wouldn't dream of it,' said Sal, taking off her school shirt to reveal the vibrant pink boob tube she'd got in the market.

Bracken was waiting for me in the usual place.

'Come and meet my friends.' I pointed to the unruly gaggle meandering down the footpath that led into town. 'We're all going to the park.' It was the first time I'd been brave enough to invite him into my world.

Bracken's face hardened. 'What, am I not enough all of a sudden?' He walked round to his side of the van and got in.

'Of course you are,' I said and reached for the passenger door to climb in beside him, but before I knew it, he'd started the engine and was driving away.

'Hey,' I shouted, running after the van. 'Wait.'

A few hundred yards up the road he stopped.

'Changed your mind?' Bracken said, smiling through the window when I drew level, like nothing'd happened. 'Jump in then.'

'I'm sorry,' I said. 'I didn't mean to hurt your feelings.'

'What you talking about?' he said, leaning across to kiss me. 'My precious Red.'

As we passed the others I kept my eyes firmly on Bracken so he'd know that if I had to choose there'd be no contest.

Chapter 13

Pete strode up and down the aisle handing out envelopes like some juvenile Father Christmas. He gave one to every girl except for me. Ever since I'd refused to look at his dad's magazines he'd cut me dead. I didn't exist.

'Swanky,' Marion waved her envelope in the air.

'Calligraphy,' Pen said, peering at the writing on the front. 'Must have a special nib.'

'La-di-da,' said Sal, staring at hers like she'd never seen her name in writing before. She opened it carefully, no ripping or tearing, to reveal a thick white card with gold print on it just like the ones Dad put on his study mantelpiece.

'Gordon Bennett,' said Pen.

'Ladies and Gents,' Sal boomed in a fake posh accent, 'Sarah and Piers Mantoni request the pleasure of your company for dinner and drinks to celebrate their son's sixteenth birthday. Dress formal.'

'What are we gonna wear?' asked Marion.

'Good excuse to go shopping,' laughed Pen.

'Do the hustle,' sang Sal, standing up and wiggling her bum.

'When is it?' I said, trying to sound nonchalant.

'You can't feel bad about not going, Cinders,' snorted Sal. 'You've got a boyfriend already.'

'She's right,' added Marion. 'You know what Pete's like. He'll only want single girls.'

I shrugged and retied my hair, trying to look like I couldn't care less while they all bleated on about what a laugh it was going to be.

At the back of the bus I could hear Pete boasting about how many girls there'd be to knob if they came. They all loved him now. Some of them even paid him to borrow his magazines overnight. When Les had found out, he'd told Pete to shove his filth where the sun didn't shine but Pete didn't care. He just carried on like the bus was his own personal fiefdom.

Fenella Jones was the only other person who wasn't invited to the party. Me and Fenella Jones in the same category. He might as well have put me in the stocks and had people throw rotten eggs at me. But the thing was I only had myself to blame. I thought back to the moment at the end of his drive; I should have just looked at his stupid mags. It wouldn't have hurt to have looked for a minute.

As we got off the bus Mary-Jane took my arm with her spindly fingers. 'Don't worry, Becs, I'm not going,' she said. 'I can't face it. Why don't you stay the night with me?'

'Thanks,' I said, wishing I could say no. Spending time with Mary-Jane was getting harder and harder. We couldn't talk about anything that mattered any more. It was all play-acting and fake. I hadn't even told her about Bracken.

The thought of the two of us hanging out in her room like we were still twelve-year-olds while everyone else was at the party felt even worse than being home on my own.

Pete's dumb party was like an itch I couldn't stop scratching. I knew I shouldn't think about it but I couldn't stop myself and the more I thought about it the worse I felt.

I shouldn't care so much but I did.

Thank God I had my evening with Bracken to prepare for. I told Dad I'd be staying with Mary-Jane, which he took in his stride. And the next time he was out, I sneaked into his room to see if there was anything of Mum's I could wear. Dad was so weird. He'd got rid of every photo of her and banned her name from being mentioned but he'd kept all her clothes.

I opened the cupboard door and a cocktail of mothballs and scent wafted out. Inside canary yellows jostled with flamingo pinks. It was a shrine to Mum's love of everything bright and alive. Dad used to take her to the King's Road, and buy her whatever she wanted. She'd come back laughing and singing, laden with 'loot' as she called it.

I pulled out a pair of gingham hot pants. I'd never dare wear them or anything else of Mum's. I wasn't brave like her.

'If you don't jump off cliffs,' she'd whispered to me, Martini in hand, 'you'll never find out whether you can fly.'

A week later she was gone.

I buried my face in the soft cashmere cardigan she'd worn the Christmas before she left and imagined she was hugging me.

Back in my bedroom I surveyed the pathetic contents of my wardrobe. Aside from my jeans, there were tweed skirts, frilly white shirts, a couple of velvet dresses and a kilt. Before long everything was piled on the floor. Nothing was right.

From the drawer by my bed, I pulled out the only photo I had of Mum. It was taken on her wedding day, in Cambridge. Dad still had hair in those days but was dressed just as he dressed now, like a real fogey in a three-piece suit with a watch on a chain. Mum looked so young next to him, although she must have been nineteen. Her hair was scooped elegantly up onto her head and she was wearing a tight, short dress even though minis hadn't come in yet. In one hand she held a cigarette in a long holder like Audrey Hepburn in *Breakfast at Tiffany's*. She was beautiful. Way out of Dad's league.

'I hope you're going to tidy that mess up,' a voice said.

I jumped guiltily and shoved the photo of Mum back in the drawer.

Mrs Turner stood in the doorway, her hands on her hips.

'I've got nothing to wear.'

'That's no excuse.'

'I look ugly and hideous in everything. I wish I was pretty.'

'Come here,' she said, putting her arms around me. 'You're plenty pretty enough. That's not your problem.' For some reason when Mrs Turner hugged me I started blubbing like a baby.

'Shush, shush,' she said gently. 'Your mum wouldn't want these tears.' We sat on the bed and I hid my face in her shoulder while she stroked my hair. 'Your dad can't help how he is. It's hard on him that you look just like your mum.'

Mrs Turner smelt of soap and talc – comforting and no nonsense – just like she had since I was little. She held me until I stopped crying and then I was embarrassed because I had snot running down my face like I was a toddler rather than someone who was nearly five foot five and about to have sex for the first time. She fished a tissue out of her sleeve and gave it to me.

'Nothing wrong with a good cry,' she said. 'Now leave it with me.' She picked up all the clothes and plonked them onto the bed. Then one by one she hung and folded each item until my room was tidy again, chatting about how her Jean had just got a job as a secretary in London. I sat on the floor cross-legged with my giant teddy and watched and listened in silence.

After she'd gone I pulled my small plastic radio from its hiding place under the bed and tried to tune into Radio Luxembourg. It hissed and crackled like it was lost at sea. Eventually I found Radio One. If I held the aerial against the metal radiator I could hear Dave Lee Travis sounding happy and a million miles away, which made me feel even more lonely. I wanted to be there, in that world, where everyone had fun and nobody got left out or had nothing to wear to go out with their new boyfriend.

The next day when I got home from school I found a black dress lying on my bed. It had lace sleeves and a soft satin body that shimmered when I moved it in the light. There was a note pinned to it in Mrs Turner's scrawly capitals: 'Jean doesn't wear it any more. Borrow it for the party.'

I slipped it on. It was a little long but I liked the way my skin peeped through the lace. It felt sexy. Grown-up. I stood on a chair so I could see the whole effect in the mirror above my chest of drawers. I didn't look like me any more and that felt good.

Chapter 14

'Flaming Nora,' Bracken said when he saw me.

I held onto his arm as he led me up Station Road. He was wearing a grey suit and crisp white shirt and his hair was brushed down flat for the first time since I'd met him. I'd borrowed Sarah Slater's black stilettos at the last minute. They were too big and too high and I teetered like a toddler who'd raided the dressing-up box.

Rockafella's was the smartest restaurant in town. A squat, mustachioed waiter with a black bow tie opened the door and a wave of warm wine-scented air wafted out.

'After you,' said Bracken.

The restaurant was full of white tablecloths and twinkling glasses and candles in wine bottles. There was a low hubbub of adult voices and cutlery clinking on china.

We were escorted to a table by the window and Bracken pulled out my chair so I could sit down. His suit was tight across his shoulders and he kept tugging at his sleeves, which finished just shy of his wrists. The menus were all in French.

We sat staring at them while the waiters circled. I had no idea what to order or whether Bracken could really afford to bring us here. If I could have waved a magic wand we'd have been ten doors down in Mick's, eating fish and chips with lots of ketchup, or at the Wimpy having burgers.

'Why don't they just have steak?' Bracken eventually asked, slapping the menu onto the table.

'Isn't that what Filet de Boeuf is?' My voice came out stiff and awkward like the cuttlefish you find wedged between the bars of a budgie's cage.

The confident chat of the other diners looped around us. A woman in a turquoise mini wove her way through the tables and stopped at ours to ask Bracken for a light. As she leant over to put her fag in the flame her skirt rode up to reveal her lacy suspenders.

Normally Bracken would be asking me what I was think-ing or getting me to tell him bits about my favourite books but tonight he didn't ask me anything. He just shifted in his chair and cleared his throat and carried on tugging at his sleeves. A couple of girls peered into the restaurant from the pavement. I straightened myself in my chair and flicked my hair back.

I'd been trying not to eat meat ever since John Lennon said animals had souls so I ordered avocado vinaigrette fol-lowed by cheese soufflé.

'Cheers,' Bracken said. He cleared his throat again and scraped his tankard against my glass. I sipped my wine and tried not to think about what Dad would say if he walked in.

The longer we went without speaking the harder it was to know what to say. It'd been just over two weeks since he'd met me at the school gates. Maybe that was as much of me as he could take.

When his steak arrived he sawed a piece off and leant over to offer me a bite. An image of a cow with big soppy eyes floated into my mind, but there was something about the way Bracken looked at me that made it impossible for me to refuse.

The silver-haired couple next door had glass dishes with balls of ice cream topped with chocolate sauce and cocktail cherries. That's what I'll order for dessert, I thought, but when the waiter asked if we wanted anything else Bracken said no without asking me. I noticed a thin layer of sweat across his forehead, which he wiped off with his napkin.

It was too terrifying to think about what was going to happen after dinner. It felt like a current had tugged me out so far from the shore that there was no way of swimming back safely.

The red candle in the centre of our table danced between us. Beside it a single rose sat in a small white china vase. I reached across to smell it only realizing as I touched the petals that it was plastic. Just then Bracken took both my hands in his.

'There's something I wanna ask you.' He stared straight into my eyes, like people never normally do in real life.

A waiter swooped in to ask about coffee, and Bracken dropped my hands, as if he'd been caught doing something wrong. He turned to the waiter like he might clock him. The waiter sidled off.

'Hot isn't it?' Bracken pulled his tie loose and undid his top button, revealing a few dark hairs at the top of his chest.

I wondered if there were more. He fumbled in his jacket pocket.

'I'd like to talk to your father.' He sounded unusually formal. 'I want him to understand I'm not like other blokes.'

'He wouldn't understand. He'd freak out and kill me so technically you'd have murdered me if you speak to him.' I couldn't tell him the truth – that Dad would never approve of him, not in a million years, whatever he said or did.

'Here,' he said, handing me a small blue box.

'What is it?'

'Open it.'

I unwound the thin white ribbon that was wrapped around it as he drained his beer glass and added, 'It's so you'll know I'm serious.'

Inside the box was a narrow silver ring with a tiny clear stone.

'It's a diamond,' he said. 'It's a bit small, but I'll get you a bigger one when I can afford it. This is just for the time being.'

I felt myself blush. 'It's beautiful,' I said.

I turned it round and the stone came alive as it caught the light. I had that horrible squirmy feeling you get when someone makes more of a fuss of you than you deserve.

'Here, allow me.' He took my left hand and slid the ring onto my wedding finger. 'I want everyone to know you're taken.'

Chapter 15

Outside the moon was full and abnormally bright as if God had forgotten to turn the lights off. We drove out beyond the station past small tangles of dark woods, through flat fields where the hedgerows shone silver in the moon's odd light. I fiddled with the ring on my finger as if it were a loose tooth, trying to work out what it meant. Were we actually engaged?

Bracken didn't say anything. He just stared straight ahead.

After a while we passed the silhouette of a large, rambling house with what looked like stables and barns attached. The rather grand pillars on either side of the front door shone white in the van's headlights.

'That,' I said, mainly because I couldn't think of anything else to say, 'is where I'd like to live when I grow up.' I pointed carelessly at the receding shape as we sped past.

'Is that right?' said Bracken. 'We'll have to see what we can do then.'

A little bit further along up a slight incline we came to a row of terraced council houses. They looked out of place perched there as if they'd been shipwrecked in the middle of the countryside. Bracken pulled up outside the house at the far end of the row.

'Not quite as smart as our neighbours, I'm afraid,' he said.

A thick wire fence ran round the small front garden.

'Mum's greyhounds,' he said, seeing me look at it. 'Doesn't want them nicked.'

He led me up the uneven path.

'Will she mind me coming back?'

'She'll be out for the count. Sleeps through anything,' he replied.

As we approached the door, from somewhere beyond the house, maybe the garden on the other side, came the sound of barking.

It was dark inside and there was the smell you'd get if you left a lot of wet dogs in a warm car. I realized it was the smell that I'd never been able to identify that was always beneath Bracken's aftershave. He took my hand and guided me over a pile of shoes and boots and up the stairs.

At the top a broken wooden gate hung. Like the kind you use to keep children in or dogs out.

Bracken's room was oblong shaped with posters of cars and girls all over the walls. An orange bulb shone from the centre of the ceiling through a paper shade. The bed had chocolate-brown sheets and was neatly made. Lined up on the floor under the window was a long row of LPs. I bent down and started flicking through them, trying to act like this was just a casual visit.

'You've got your books,' he said, lighting a green triangular candle with a zippo, 'and I have my music. That's where I do my learning.'

The albums were arranged in perfect alphabetical order starting with Baez, Black Sabbath, Bowie and Bread through the Eagles, Genesis, the Grateful Dead, Jethro Tull, Kiss and Pink Floyd to Led Zep, which he stored under Z rather than L. I pulled out the latest Stones, *Black and Blue*.

'Stand up,' he said, pulling me to my feet. 'I've already chosen.'

'Shall I read you a new poem I found? I've brought it in my bag.' I was suddenly desperate to delay whatever was going to happen.

Bracken shook his head. 'Afterwards.'

He leant over the player and lowered the needle onto a single that was already there. 'Nights in White Satin', the first song we danced to together, started playing. He turned to face me.

For what felt like ages he just stood there staring at me with the music playing and me standing there with my heart pounding, feeling like my legs might give way at any moment out of fear of what was going to happen next.

'Turn round,' he eventually instructed.

I turned.

He tugged the zip at the back of my dress. I'd imagined him stroking the lace sleeves, smoothing the satin with his fingers, but he just wanted it off. The dress fell in a circle around my feet.

He turned me back around and looked at me some more. I felt foolish in my flowery bra and sensible knickers. Mrs Turner bought all my underwear so I didn't have anything sexy to choose from. I thought of the girls on *Miss World* and how they twirled confidently in their bikinis as their vital statistics were read out. Maybe if I had a *Miss World* figure I'd know how to stand but right now I just wanted Bracken to blow the candle out. I didn't want him to be able to see my flat chest and skinny hips.

When he'd done with looking at me he started to take his clothes off. He did it efficiently like it was how he did it every day. First his socks, then his shirt and then his trousers. He folded them all neatly in a pile on the floor. I turned away so he wouldn't think I was watching. A girly calendar hung from the back of the closed door. Miss March looked out at me cradling her huge boobs with their dark-brown nipples. I wished I could disappear. A line of poetry popped into my head, *fade far away and quite forget.* That's what I wanted to do but instead I stood there like an idiot in my white cotton pants in a strange coffin-shaped room that smelt of greyhounds and aftershave.

'Lie down.' Bracken motioned to the bed.

I lay down and soon he was lying beside me and we were kissing and once we were kissing everything felt safe and okay again like we were just in his garage or parked in a lay-by on the way home from school. Only we weren't.

My body jolted as his bare skin brushed against mine. And then it started to hum and feel fuzzy all over.

This is it, I thought, it's going to happen.

He unfastened my bra and unlooped it over my arms. I closed my eyes to try to make myself invisible. I felt his hands run through my hair and tug my head back, deep into the pillow. He leant over me and his lips sucked and pulled at mine.

His skin felt poker-hot as he lowered himself on top of me. I closed my eyes more tightly and felt his teeth graze against my neck and then the heat of his hand as it slid slowly down my stomach and into my knickers.

He rested his hand between my legs and gently pressed his fingers into me. I felt stiff, awkward, scared like I wouldn't live up to his expectations in some way.

When he lifted my hips up and slid my knickers down and off my legs I was relieved: he did still like me.

He started kissing me more frantically. Licking and pulling at my lips and shoving his tongue deep inside my mouth.

Then, with his legs he pushed mine apart. Wide. This really is it, I thought, as I felt him free himself from his pants. At first he just held himself against me and then he started to push. Softly at first and then harder and harder.

'Give me some help,' he whispered, but I had no idea how to help or what to do and suddenly the magic was gone and I was just scared and rigid and wanting to scream for help and run away.

'Wider,' he said, putting his fingers into his mouth. 'Open your legs wider.' His fingers smeared wet onto me, prised into me. But my legs were as wide as they could be and my body was still resisting. He pushed harder, moving backwards and forwards, stabbing and jerking against me. His sweat splotched in beads down onto me.

'Relax,' he whispered. Raising himself up on his hands, he peeled his chest away from mine so I lay exposed beneath him. 'Open your eyes,' he insisted. 'Look at me.'

I didn't.

'Red, it's me, Bracken, I'm not going to hurt you.'

I couldn't open my eyes. I couldn't. I didn't want to see him seeing me, looking at me lying there naked and stupid and scrawny and scared.

'Hey,' he whispered, kissing each of my closed eyes gently. 'Let's take a breather. I don't want you to do anything you're not ready for.'

He rolled back onto the bed beside me, his body tacky with sweat, like an athlete mid-race. I didn't know what had gone wrong, why it hadn't worked. Maybe he wasn't trying in the right place or maybe he was too big to fit.

I thought back to when I'd first tried to use a tampon. I'd stood behind the locked bathroom door for hours trying to shove it inside me, not knowing where exactly it should go, terrified I'd be the only girl in school left using sanitary towels. Maybe I was right to panic then. Maybe there was something fundamentally and totally wrong with my body.

Grown-ups made it sound like it was so easy to lose your virginity. Like it was the kind of thing you could discard by accident. Well, not me. I'd failed even at that.

I lay in the dark waiting for Bracken to tell me we were over, to ask for the ring back, to make me get my stuff and go home, tell me that I was just a pathetic schoolgirl. Once he'd got rid of me he'd be able to find someone else, no problem. Someone experienced who'd know how to do it.

Just as I was about to start crying and make an even bigger fool of myself he reached across and took my hand. He held it for a moment and then took it and put it on his thing.

'You don't mind, do you?' he asked.

The surface felt strange, soft suede or maybe dry moss on bark, not at all how I'd thought it would feel. I didn't look down.

I had no clue what to do with it other than hold it, so that's what I did. Held it and squeezed it ever so gently.

Bracken started nibbling my ear and then put a rough palm on each of my breasts, like he was comparing them. I wanted to run or just grab the covers and hide and not come out ever, but this was my opportunity to make things right. He was giving me a second chance.

As his hands perched domed over each of my teeny breasts, I remembered Dom saying how a girl he'd felt up had had poached eggs instead of melons. I looked at Miss March over on the door with her ginormous tits and her dinner-plate nipples. When I was cold mine were no bigger than raisins.

'They're sweet,' he whispered, sucking on my ear and squeezing each breast in turn. Then he twisted and tugged each nipple so they were hard. It hurt but my body started to respond. He nestled his head into the crook of my neck and I heard him groan very softly.

'Just do this for a moment.' He took my hand and made it grip his thing harder and then he made my hand move up and down so that the skin shifted backwards and forwards.

After a few minutes I stopped, thinking he might get bored if I kept doing the same thing to it over and over again.

'Don't stop,' he said. 'Not now.'

So I started again and a few moments later his breath quickened and then I felt his whole body shudder and arch like he was yawning, only he wasn't, he was biting my neck and gasping and then I felt something warm and sticky seep out through my fingers.

'God I needed that,' he groaned. 'You've had me on the edge since I first danced with you.'

He took a corner of the sheet and gently wiped my hand clean. I put my head on his shoulder and he kissed the top of my head. I felt a rush of satisfaction that I'd done something right. I allowed my fingers to explore the smattering of hairs on his chest, they were soft, not like the bristles on his chin, and I could feel the ridge of his ribs beneath them and beneath that very softly the beat of his heart.

Within minutes his breath had slowed and he'd drifted off to sleep. Outside a car whizzed past the open window. I felt a surge of homesickness, the same feeling you get when you're little and staying at somebody's house for the first time. I tried to pull the covers up over us to make it more cosy but I couldn't move them without waking him.

Twisting the engagement ring on my finger I thought about what Mary-Jane or her mother or even Pen or Marion would say if they knew where I was. I went through all the names we'd called Sarah's big sister when we knew she'd had it off with someone. Slag, slut, nympho, tramp, easy. Mrs Hamilton wouldn't use those words; she'd just say I'd let myself down.

Soon after that it dawned on me: I wasn't going to be able to tell anyone about what was going on between me and Bracken. None of them would get it. They'd just think it was a juicy bit of gossip to be traded in the playground. They wouldn't understand this was something different. I couldn't tell a soul. It was going to have to be my secret.

Chapter 16

Dad cleared his throat and ran a hand across his shiny pate like he'd forgotten he didn't have any hair. He was wearing his tuxedo.

'I seem to have acquired two tickets to hear the village operatic society mutilate *The Mikado* tonight. I thought you might accompany me. It could prove entertaining.'

'Entertaining,' I spluttered. Everyone else was going to be at Pete's party, it would be the end of everything if anyone saw me out in town with my Dad dressed like a penguin.

Dad fumbled in his cigar box and for the first time I can remember he looked hurt. Music was what he'd used to do with Mum. It was their thing.

'Dad, I'd love to, but Mary-Jane's expecting me again tonight.'

Dad held his silver Dunhill lighter up to his cigar and took a series of short sharp puffs, till the smoke billowed like a train about to leave the station.

'Can we go another time?' I ventured.

With his glasses at the end of his nose and cigar smoke all around him he suddenly looked helpless, like a mole emerging from a burrow on a foggy day. I wondered what would happen if I went over and hugged him.

'I'll cancel her. Can I use the phone?'

I went out to the kitchen and dialled her number. Engaged. Mrs Hamilton was probably gassing. I dialled again. This could be good after all; Dad might even let me ask him about Mum.

'Won't be long,' I shouted to Dad.

I kept dialling and redialling the number. Maybe I should call the operator and have her interrupt the call. I drew a large 'B' on the pad and twisted the yellow cord round the pencil. 7pm. I dialled again. They'd normally be having dinner by now. I wondered what time the show started.

From the study I could hear the chorus of 'Three Little Maids from School' belting out from the record player. I tried one last time.

'Come and reacquaint yourself with the melodies,' called Dad.

He looked like he was off to a wedding – he'd put a bow tie on and had a silk scarf around his neck. He lifted the needle and moved it to his favourite track. With his whisky in one hand and beating time with the other he sang, *Tit willow tit willow tit willow*. It sounded so embarrassing. I couldn't possibly go with him.

'I can't get through. Mary-Jane's expecting me. What should I do?'

'You seem to live with that family. It's a wonder they don't charge you room and board. There is such a thing as moderation, Rebecca. Overstaying your welcome. One evening with your father won't kill you.'

'But she's not very well, Dad. Since the, you know. Can't you go with someone else? Or just go on your own? I'm sorry, Dad, I can't let her down.'

Dad turned the record player off. 'I won't be lied to.'

'I'm not lying. You try her number and see.'

'You're honestly expecting me to believe your reluctance is due to a prior arrangement with Mary-Jane?' He refilled his glass from the decanter and sat down at his desk.

'Yes. I'm trying to cancel it, I just can't get through.'

He took his cigar from the ashtray, relit it and then leant forward across his desk like he was delivering the closing argument in court. 'Mrs Turner seems to think you'll be attending a party at the Mantonis tonight.'

'No way.'

'I'd like the truth.'

'I *am* telling the truth.'

'If you're lying, Rebecca…' He tapped his cigar on the crystal ashtray. 'I won't have you at that place. Understand?'

'Well, you don't need to worry. I'm not even invited.'

'I'm delighted to hear that.'

His copy of *The Times* lay next to the ashtray. On the front page was a picture of Concorde taking off. Perhaps it was flying to America and maybe that's where Mum was.

'Too much money, Rebecca. Vulgar.' A button on his dress shirt had come undone and I could see the grey-white flesh of his tummy. His face was flushed. I suddenly felt frightened that he was going to die. Soon.

'Can I use the phone again, Dad? Try to get through? If

it's still engaged we could just drop by on the way and tell her.'

'The moment has passed,' he said and picked up his newspaper. 'The moment is dead and gone,' he repeated.

From outside in the garden I heard the sound of the sprinkler.

'What about your homework?' he asked from behind *The Times*.

'Done,' I lied.

'Why don't you show it to me?'

'Because I'm not a child any more.' I stormed out of the room.

Later, when I crept back down to go to Mary-Jane's I assumed he'd be passed out in his chair but he stepped out of the study and blocked the hall. He'd taken off his jacket and bow tie and his remaining strands of hair had fallen forward so he resembled an upmarket Worzel Gummidge.

'You okay, Dad?' I tried to sound light-hearted.

'You cannot go out looking like that.'

'What do you mean?'

I was wearing my jeans and white shirt. Same as always.

A film of saliva glistened on Dad's bottom lip like he'd forgotten to swallow. He reached out to grab hold of me and I heard my shirt rip as I pushed past him and out of the door.

Chapter 17

Of course, Mary-Jane was in her room. I don't know why I'd hoped it would be different like she might be downstairs ready to come to the pub or do something fun.

Her mum greeted me at the door. 'Thank God you've come, Becs. MJ has been so looking forward to your visit. She's still not herself.'

'We're all really worried about her,' I said, hoping she wouldn't see I'd been crying.

Instead of letting me go upstairs, Mrs Hamilton led me into the kitchen. Sitting on the table was a plate of fairy cakes decorated with thick creamy icing and sprinkled with multi-coloured hundreds and thousands.

'I made these for you two,' she said, gesturing to the cakes. 'Let's have a quick cuppa before we take them upstairs.'

Mrs Hamilton always used to let Mary-Jane and me have hot sweet tea in real china cups while she and my mum chatted. I sat down at the wooden table and rubbed my bare feet against the prickly rush matting.

'I blame myself,' Mrs Hamilton was saying. 'If I hadn't gone to work when she was little...'

'You needed to work,' I protested. From the sitting room next door I could hear Benny Hill on the TV and Mr Hamilton laughing.

'I've packed it in.' She pulled a pack of Kents out of a drawer in the table. 'MJ needs me and that's more important.'

I didn't know what to say. She loved her job and I didn't know she smoked. It didn't seem like Mrs Hamilton's thing at all.

'She seems to be a lot better.' I tried to sound confident. 'She's back at school.'

'Gerald always said I should give up work when I had MJ.' There was a ring of pink lipstick around her cigarette filter, which she tried to smudge off with her fingers. 'But I thought it would be good for MJ to learn that women can work, have a career too, you know, make something more of ourselves.' She seemed to have forgotten all about the cup of tea and was now pouring herself a glass of red wine from the box on the counter.

'We were all jealous of Mary-Jane,' I said, 'having a mum like you. You're so glamorous.'

'Really?'

'And you make the best cakes.'

Mrs Hamilton smiled and squeezed my hand. 'Thanks, Rebecca. The thing is, it's not over yet. Those bloody police.' She paused to drink some more wine. 'Can I tell you something in confidence?'

'Of course.'

'Promise you won't tell MJ? I don't want her to worry about it till it happens.'

I nodded my head.

'You know she blames herself, don't you? Thinks he must have chosen her because there's something wrong with her.'

I nodded again although the truth was Mary-Jane hadn't said a word about it, not to any of us.

Mrs Hamilton took my hand. 'It's so good MJ has a friend like you. Thank God for you,' she said. 'The thing is, though, what happened is worse than anybody thinks. He did more than touch her, you know, he…'

All of a sudden Mrs Hamilton was crying with her face puckered like a young girl, her mascara running. I put my arms around her and rested my head on hers.

'Oh Becs, I don't want you worrying about me,' she sniffed. 'You haven't exactly had an easy time. It just all feels so unfair. What's MJ ever done to anyone?' She fished a hankie out of her sleeve and dabbed at her eyes. 'They want her to do an identity parade.'

I nodded. I'd heard Dad talk about them.

A bit of ash dropped onto the table as she took a long drag on her fag. 'They said she's got to go to the police station and look at all the men they've found. It's the only way they can be sure they get the right person.' She rubbed a finger into the ash, smearing it into the wooden surface. 'I don't know how she'll cope. But if she doesn't try that dreadful man will be free to do it again to any of you.'

'She'll be fine,' I said. 'We'll take care of her. Please don't worry.'

'I know you will, Becs,' she said and patted my arm.

'Shall I ask Dad?' I added. 'You know, maybe there's something legal he can do. Maybe she could get out of it? I could ask him.'

'That's very kind, darling. I know I could ask your father myself but I think we're all right for now. He has enough on his plate. How are things between you now anyway, and what on earth has happened to your shirt?'

'Ripped it,' I said. 'Brambles.'

'Let me have it.' She stood up. 'I'll have it stitched in no time. It's your favourite, isn't it? Cheesecloth. I should get one like this for MJ.'

'Thanks,' I said and waited while she fetched one of Mary-Jane's T-shirts from the laundry. When she came back she made me raise my arms so she could slip my shirt off over my head. Then she gave me the T-shirt to put on.

'Can't have you in tatters.' She handed me the plate of fairy cakes to take up to Mary-Jane.

Chapter 18

Mary-Jane didn't look as if she'd moved since the last time I was there. She was sitting on the bed with her knees bent up under her chin, wearing a woolly fisherman's jumper and knee-length socks pulled up over the legs of her jeans. She started slightly as I entered the room.

'Thanks for coming,' she said, smiling unconvincingly. 'I'm so bored of sitting here.'

'Well, why don't we go out then?' I said. 'Come on, I'll look after you.'

Her bottom lip started to wobble. 'I can't really face it yet.'

'Come on, please. Just try.'

Mary-Jane shook her head.

'Do you want to talk? You know, about what happened? It might help.'

Mary-Jane shook her head again.

'What then? Do you want me to read something? Or we could go for a walk to the pond.'

Her shelves were full of pony annuals and jigsaw puzzles. One of her mum's silk scarves hung across the mirror on the dressing table and her drawing things were out in front of it. I picked up her sketchbook – she'd been drawing masses of tiny spirals, all on top of each other in thick black pen. I wished she'd come to the pub.

'We could listen to music,' she suggested.

'What have you got?' I shrugged.

'Everything we recorded.' She sprang off her bed like the Mary-Jane she used to be and went to the window. 'I haven't wiped any of them.'

Behind the green Laura Ashley curtain was a neat row of cassette tapes. Some were albums but most were recordings she'd made straight off the radio with her neat handwriting on the spine. I thought of Bracken's stack of LPs and wished I was there lying in bed with him listening to his music. I scoured the options: David Essex, the Osmonds, the Bay City Rollers, Barry Manilow and her home-made comps.

'Here,' she said, handing me one. 'It's got 10cc three minutes in. Or that one's got Bowie on if you want?' She plugged her radio cassette player into the socket by the door and rested it on her desk.

I could see she was trying to please me and I felt guilty so I let her put the 10cc one on because that was her favourite. She fast-forwarded to 'I'm Mandy, Fly Me', which she adored because it was about an air hostess like her mum. When it was released we'd made up this dance routine where we acted out the whole song line by line.

'Shall we practise?'

I felt sort of stupid doing it now but I couldn't face

disappointing her. We pushed her desk chair out of the way so there was enough room on the floor for both of us. I stood beside her and started the moves. When it got to *I'm Mandy, fly me* we both stuck our arms out like we were aeroplanes and turned in circles. I started to giggle as the whole thing felt ridiculous; I couldn't believe we used to do this so seriously. Mary-Jane started to giggle too and soon we were both zooming around the room laughing and shrieking the lyrics. When the track finished we rewound it and did the whole thing again and then again. For half an hour or longer it was like nothing had changed, like Mary-Jane hadn't been attacked and got scarily thin and like we were still so close we could virtually read each other's minds.

Then the tape started making a weird squeaking noise like it was about to get eaten, so Mary-Jane swopped it for another of her comps. We collapsed puffed out onto the bed, closed our eyes and sang along to 'American Pie' in cheesy American accents. Then she fast-forwarded to 'You Sexy Thing' and leapt up again and started doing the moves we'd worked out for it. I tried to join in but it was the song I'd danced to the night I met Bracken. It was his song now, not hers. It was his and mine together. I looked at Mary-Jane and felt embarrassed by her childishness.

'Let's have a rest,' I said and turned the player off. 'Here, eat one of your mum's fairy cakes.'

'Don't you like doing that any more?' She was giving me her wounded puppy-dog look.

'I'm just tired.' I sounded cross without meaning to. 'Budge up.' I perched beside her on the bed, giving her a gentle shove. She shuffled across so we could both sit side by side.

'Can I tell you something?' I asked. 'Something totally secret?'

'Of course. Swear.' She slipped her arm through mine.

'I've met someone,' I said. 'I don't mean someone, anyone. I mean the "one". I've met the "one". You know, like we each always hoped we would.'

'What, already? Becs, that's so amazing. Is that why you've been acting so different?'

'I'm not different.'

'Becs, you're acting all tough and hard, but it doesn't matter.' She took my hand. 'It doesn't matter at all so long as you're okay. Happy.'

'He's been picking me up from school. Have any of the others said anything?'

She shook her head.

I started to tell her about Bracken. About the night we met, about how I went to the pub and he was just there, standing by the bar. 'Like fate had just put him there, waiting for me to come in,' I said. 'And that's what he thinks too. That it was all predestined. Meant to be.' I paused for a second, wondering which bit to tell her next. And then I started thinking about last night, about how we actually slept in the same bed together, naked all night.

'What night was it?' Mary-Jane asked. 'That you met him.'

'The fifteenth.' And then I realized why she was asking.

'That's the same night, Becs. I can't. I can't hear about it. While you were out there with him I was at the station and all those police officers were asking me horrible questions like "Did you do anything to make him stop his van?" And then they wanted to examine me and Dad started shouting at

them and they got aggressive back. Becs, I just can't…' She
started crying and I put my arms around her and held her,
letting her sob into my chest, her tears seeping through the
borrowed T-shirt. I let her sob until she couldn't sob any
longer.

As she stretched a long arm across my chest I saw her skin
was covered in lots of tiny white hairs almost like down.
'I want you to be happy, very happy. It's just that…'

I kissed the top of her blonde head. 'You don't need to say
anything.'

We sat like that for a long time, in total silence. Her breath
steadied and her body softened as she fell asleep.

Gently I freed myself from her arm and slid off the bed.

'Don't go,' she stirred. 'Becs. Stay.'

'You need to sleep,' I whispered.

'I don't.' She reached out for my hand. 'Please stay.'

'I can't. Dad'll be worried about me.'

I bent down to hug her and she shifted her weight as I
lifted the covers up from under her so she could slide down
into the bed while I tucked her in.

'Don't change too much,' she said as I kissed her good
night. 'I mean change but just not too much.'

I met Mrs Hamilton coming up the stairs as I was on my
way down. 'Here,' she said handing me my shirt, 'it's as good
as new.'

'Thanks.' I could smell wine and cigarettes on her breath
and she still had a blob of mascara on one cheek.

'Come back again soon,' she called after me.

Chapter 19

As I cycled past Pete's driveway a long black limo pulled into it, sleek and shiny, the kind of car a pop star like Bryan Ferry or Marc Bolan would travel in. I watched its tail lights disappear up the drive. In the distance I could hear voices and music and through the trees green and red disco lights flashed. The party. I'd actually forgotten all about it.

I hid my bike behind some bushes and without really meaning to I found myself walking through the large wooden gates at the start of the front drive.

I crept along, following the curve of the poplar trees that lined it.

The woods just beyond the verge looked spooky and laced with danger so I stuck to the drive despite the risk of someone seeing me. The crunch of my feet on the thick gravel sounded impossibly loud and the white of my shirt made me way too visible.

I jumped as a particularly large stick snapped underfoot.

I thought about turning back but the flashing lights and the rhythmic thump of the disco were too much to resist.

As the drive bent sharply to the right I saw the house for the first time. It was lit by hundreds of tiny lights and was ginormous like an ocean liner or the fairytale castle at the start of Walt Disney films. Dad was right, they must be loaded. But it didn't look vulgar to me; it looked like a life I'd like to be part of. It looked fantastic.

The woods gave way to fields so that there was now a large expanse of open grass between me and the house. I could hear Frankie Valli singing 'Oh, What a Night' and every few seconds the flash of a strobe as bright as lightning revealed the silhouettes of people dancing inside a giant marquee. As I got nearer still I could hear shrieks and screams and splashes, which must have been coming from the pool.

In the field to the left of the drive directly in front of the house were rows of neatly parked cars like you get at a gym-khana or a village cricket match. Two blokes in yellow vests with torches directed the traffic.

I should've turned back but something inside me insisted on seeing what I was missing. I reasoned that that way, at least, when they were all telling their stories on the bus I wouldn't feel so left out – I'd have seen it for myself.

I cut across the field so I could use the parked cars as cover. I broke into a jog and found myself laughing as I ran – what on earth was I doing? I ducked down behind an E-Type Jaguar. Just ahead the door of a Range Rover clunked shut and I heard a woman's voice say, 'It's so typical of Piers. What's he going to do when his son turns eighteen, for Christ's sake?'

'Fly us all to Monte Carlo, I hope,' replied a man.

I picked my way forward, keeping low, wary of the blokes with the torches. There was a Bentley, a Mercedes and even a Rolls. There were a few old bangers too, but not many. I wondered how people like Sal and Sarah had got out here, as none of their parents had cars.

I decided to follow the hedge that surrounded the garden until I got to the pool. I could hear shrieks and splashes and laughter.

The pool itself was surrounded by a thick slatted fence so I couldn't actually see what was happening. I was so busy trying to peek over the fence that I almost tripped over a guy who was sitting on the grass.

'What you up to, babe?' he asked. 'Dig the way you're not doing the whole dress thing.' He was wearing a dinner jacket and was drinking from a jug.

'Want some?' he offered.

'All right.' I sat down on the grass beside him.

I took a swig. I couldn't see what I was drinking but it had bits of apple and what tasted like cucumber floating in it.

'Vile, isn't it?' said the guy. 'It's all I could get. The vodka was behind the bar, but the Pimm's was just sitting on the table.'

'Better than nothing,' I said and took another sip.

'Harry,' he said, stretching out on the grass so his hand reached mine. His voice was like Pete's, lazy, confident.

'Rebecca,' I said and then wished I'd given a false name. 'I'm not meant to be here,' I blurted.

'Wish I wasn't, only came 'cos of Father. He went to school with Piers,' drawled Harry. 'Don't worry, I won't grass you up. Talking of grass, do you want some?'

He didn't wait for my answer but lay back and rooted about in his pockets. 'Take a look at those stars,' he said. I couldn't work out whether he was drunk or just super relaxed. He certainly wasn't shy like me.

'So what's a nice girl like you doing sneaking into a party like this?'

'I'm at school with Pete,' I started, but he interrupted before I'd worked out how to explain.

'Well, you'd better watch out,' he said. 'Hope he's cleaned up his act. Pretty sorry mess he made of Harrow. Lucky his dad was rich enough to keep it out of the papers.'

'What happened?' I asked.

Just as he was about to tell me a girl in a shiny pink sleeveless dress tottered by.

'Hey babe, wanna join us?' Harry called out to her. 'Oh it's Laura. Stunning outfit.'

Laura crouched down beside him. 'Got any fags, Hal?' she asked. 'I'm gasping.' They kissed each other on both cheeks with a loud lip-smacking sound. Her hair was blonde and pinned up in a fancy do with pin curls that hung down on either side of her face making her look famous like Twiggy.

Harry produced some Sobranies from his inside pocket. 'Allow me,' he said, sitting up and shielding the flame from his lighter as she inhaled. 'Haven't seen you since that thing at the Dorchester. Where've you been hiding yourself?'

'Long story,' she said and sat down in the space between Harry and me. Her bony back curved towards me as she chattered away to him about having to be a chalet girl for a season and how ghastly it was. I kept waiting for Harry to say something or introduce me and bring me into the conversation but he didn't. I felt a sudden surge of embarrassment. What on earth was I doing here? What would happen if Sal or Dom or any of the others saw me?

As I crept away there were still people arriving. Another blonde woman tiptoed by in ridiculous heels, arm in arm with a man in an evening suit. I still had the warm taste of the Pimm's in my mouth. This whole party was disgusting and so was everyone in it. All I wanted to do was get home.

I set off back the way I'd come. As I approached the car park I saw a group of people gathered round a low-slung sports car. The bonnet was up and two car-park attendants were shining torches on the engine while a third man fiddled with it. I stooped down level with the roofs of the other cars so I wouldn't be seen and crept closer. A girl with a feather boa was explaining to anyone who would listen that it always started first time.

The man who was bent over the engine stood up.

'Battery. That's all,' he announced in a familiar voice. 'Give me a sec and it'll be right as rain.'

It was then that I saw Bracken's van parked behind the sports car. I watched as he walked round to the back of it. Every bit of me wanted to run over to him. How amazing that he should be here too. Fate, he'd call it. But just as I was about to call out his name I thought of the girl in the boa and Harry and Laura and everyone else standing around, and what they'd think if I ran over and hugged the break-down man, and so I didn't go over to him or say anything. I just snuck home.

Chapter 20

A string of burgundy-coloured love bites trailed from Sal's shoulder to her neck. She'd finally got off with Dom and looked like she'd been mauled by a vampire.

'Why don't you put toothpaste on them?' asked Marion.

'Because I don't want to smell like a toothbrush,' snapped Sal.

It was clear Sal didn't really want to sit with us on the bus any more; she'd rather have been with Dom. But Dom was down the back with the boys and probably already boasting about how easy Sal was. She'd never have let him get very far but that wouldn't stop him.

I slipped the tip of my finger into Bracken's ring, which I'd pinned out of sight inside my skirt pocket. Its shape felt certain, comforting. I should have gone up to him last night. I was a coward.

'He was so pissed,' Pen explained, 'that they had to call his dad to come and get him and now his parents are furious with Pete's parents for having so much booze around.'

'Who?' I couldn't stop myself asking.

'Phil,' said Sal. 'He's still in bed now.'

'You could drink as much as you wanted,' said Marion. 'Anything. All on tap. No one cared what we did and they had real waiters with silver trays and bow ties. The works.'

'The best bit was the swimming, though, wasn't it?' said Pen. 'The pool had lights under the water.'

'It was dead romantic,' Sal added, batting her eyelashes like she thought she was Marilyn Monroe. 'We were literally dancing under the stars when Dom made his move on me.'

'What about Sarah Slater, though?' said Marion. 'When I went to get my coat she was lying on the bed.'

'So?' I sounded sceptical.

'Guess who was on top of her?' Marion looked like she was about to explode with excitement.

'Who?'

'No, you've got to guess,' insisted Marion. 'They had their clothes on but they were completely glued together.'

'Just tell,' I ordered. Marion always gave in if you were firm enough.

'Pete,' said Marion. 'Sarah Slater got off with Pete. What's more he's really into her.'

'Yeah, look at them,' Pen pointed behind her. 'They can't leave each other alone.'

Sure enough a few rows from the back Pete and Sarah were sitting with their arms round each other. It was first thing on Monday morning but that wasn't stopping them. They were snogging like they were a honeymoon couple on a desert island.

'He's loaded,' whispered Pen. 'You wouldn't have believed their house, would she, Marion?'

I stared out the window while they went on and on about it, feeling invisible.

Then I remembered what Mary-Jane's mum had told me. I waited till Pen had told the story of finding Sarah Slater on the bed for the third time and Sal had refused for the fifth time to answer Marion about whether she'd marry Dom if he asked her, and then I slipped in, 'By the way, any of you heard the latest about Mary-Jane?'

'No, what?' demanded Sal.

Pen stood up and scanned the bus for her. 'I hope nothing else's happened to her.'

'I saw her.' I made it sound like I'd just run into her in the street or the shop, something casual. I didn't want them to think I hadn't had anything better to do while they were at Pete's.

'It's top secret,' I continued. 'Her mum doesn't want anyone to know.'

'Come on,' said Sal. 'Spill it.' Which was rich coming from her, as she was the one who milked everything.

'They might have found him,' I said.

'Who?' asked Marion.

'The perv,' snapped Sal. 'Have you got a brain?'

'Shut up.' Marion shoved a sharp elbow into her ribs.

'Who is it then?' Pen sounded dubious.

'I don't know,' I replied, 'but it all depends on Mary-Jane. They don't want anyone to know but they're going to make her do an identity parade.'

'So what?' said Sal. 'They always do that.'

'Poor Mary-Jane,' said Pen. 'She'll have to stare him in the face.'

'What is it anyway?' asked Marion.

'Oh for Christ's sake,' snapped Sal.

From the back of the bus Dom shouted out, 'Oy Sal, get down here.'

'Who do you think you are?' Sal shouted back, but she got up all the same and slowly wiggled her way back to join him. Soon everyone was talking about Pete's party again and how there was a photographer who was taking photos for some glossy magazine.

That afternoon Bracken picked me up as usual. Lou Reed's 'Perfect Day' was playing full blast as he drove me, with the windows down, to the park where we joined the queue of jostling kids and worn-out mums at the ice-cream van. He slung his arm across my shoulders like I was his personal property. Two boys in front of us were fighting, bored with the wait, but I couldn't care less. This moment could last forever and it would be enough, I'd die happy.

'You haven't noticed,' said Bracken. 'Maybe I didn't get it big enough.'

'What?'

He took his arm from around my shoulders and presented his bicep for inspection.

'It's muscly,' I said.

'Not that,' he said. 'Try again.'

He lifted the sleeve of his Led Zep T-shirt and then I saw it. A red heart with an arrow piercing it. Inside the heart in black was written 'R 4 B' and underneath that 'Till Death Do Us Part' in italics.

'I put R instead of B for you because I thought the R could stand for Red and Rebecca. I know we're not married yet but I thought it could be my version of an engagement ring.'

'Is it permanent?' I asked.

'Of course it is, you idiot.' Bracken laughed. 'Like it says, "Till Death Do Us Part". It'll be on my arm till the end.'

I ran my finger gently over the raised skin. In my head I could hear Dad's voice saying that only thugs and hooligans had tattoos.

'It must've hurt,' I said.

'You've got to suffer to be beautiful. Not everyone's born beautiful like you, Red.'

'Shut up,' I squealed, thumping him on his arm.

'Ouch,' he screamed. 'Not there.'

'You two are as bad as my boys,' said the mum in front of us in the queue.

'Sorry,' I said.

'Enjoy it while it lasts,' she smiled.

'It will last,' Bracken said sharply. Turning to face me he angled my chin up towards him. 'I don't want to waste a second of my life with you.'

He lifted his shades to the top of his head so that I was staring into his deep-brown eyes and then he started to kiss me. Not little gentle pecks but full, proper kissing. For an instant I was scared. What if Dad or someone who knew him saw us? What if Mrs Turner or one of the teachers at school drove by? But he wouldn't let me pull away and within seconds of his lips touching mine I'd stopped thinking about everything except for Bracken and his sweet taste and the heat our bodies made when they were clasped together.

'Naughty, naughty,' said a familiar voice. Dom thwacked me on the bum.

I pulled back and wiped my mouth, embarrassed. 'You getting ice creams too?' I asked.

'No, going to the park with my missus.'

Beside him Sal was standing with a stupid smirk on her face. She was carrying a plastic bag and I could see it had a bottle of Strongbow inside. 'Quick or we'll be left behind,' she said to Dom. She didn't say anything to me or even look at Bracken.

They walked off into the park hand in hand and just ahead of them I saw Pete and Sarah Slater.

A second later Marion and Pen passed by.

'Watcha,' said Marion.

'This is Bracken,' I said to them.

Marion blushed.

'Watcha,' said Pen and then before there was time to start a conversation with them she'd got Marion by the arm and was saying, 'Hurry up.' They didn't ask us to come too but just trotted off like pathetic puppies behind the others.

'Is that your gang?' asked Bracken.

'Used to be,' I replied.

Chapter 21

When it finally happened I was sitting on the kitchen counter next to a set of striped blue-and-white jars containing sugar and flour and tea. A pack of the dogs' mince lay open on the table and a small halo of flies hovered above it. Bracken's mum was out at the greyhound track so we had the house to ourselves.

Bracken came up to me, reached under my grey school skirt and tugged my knickers off.

'Oy,' I said. 'Manners.'

'Shh,' he said and pushed my legs apart. 'You behave.' And while his tongue sought out mine he was unzipping his jeans and trying again. I wished we could just kiss, I loved his kisses. I'd have been so happy if that's all we ever did. But I wasn't an idiot and I knew that if I didn't let him go further sooner or later he'd get frustrated and chuck me for someone else or find a bit on the side.

'Wait there a mo.' Bracken disappeared into the lounge and returned with a cushion from the sofa, which he slid underneath me.

'That's better.' He ran his tongue up my neck. 'Can't have you being uncomfortable.' He pulled me forward on the counter so I was right at the edge and then pushed my legs wide apart again.

I wanted to ask him if he needed to get a johnny but I was too shy. We'd talked about it once before and he'd said he'd never got anyone pregnant so I wouldn't need to worry.

One of the flies had landed on the meat, which had started to turn grey from the heat of the day. I wanted to say please can we not do it here. It had been romantic lying down in his room with a candle and a slow album playing and a drink or two. But here on the counter didn't feel right. It was too clinical. I started to panic.

'Please just wait,' I whispered.

'Hang on a sec,' he said, pushing himself hard against me, and then it was too late.

The bolt of pain bit into me. I tried to shove him back but he held me tight against him so I couldn't move.

'It's all right,' he whispered. 'It won't hurt for long.' And then he carried on pushing deeper moving in and out of me and it rubbed where the pain was inside of me and after a while it was hurting so much I had to bite my hand so that I wouldn't scream out. When he was finished he let out this low moan.

'Red. That was fantastic.' He snuggled his head into the crook of my neck and kissed me, his stubble prickling my skin. The thump of his heart hard against his ribcage made me think of the time a bird had flown straight thwack into Dad's windscreen.

He was still inside me. I rested my head on top of his and

looked out across the stack of plates in the sink through the window to the dry brown fields beyond and thought this is it; I've really done it.

A wave of fear started to bubble and then rise inside me. What had just happened was irreversible, permanent. It couldn't ever be undone. I buried my face in Bracken's thick messy hair. This was what I'd wanted, I reminded myself, what I'd chosen. This was what proper, grown-up love was.

After ages of us just staying like that, locked together, him leaning against me and me breathing in his familiar smell I finally started to relax and when I did a strange almost euphoric sense of relief flowed through me. It was done. Decided. We were joined. One.

Eventually, he shifted his weight. 'Let's go upstairs and lie down together.'

I pulled him back. 'Don't move. I don't want time to start ticking again.'

'I've got to, Becs,' he said and kissed my forehead. 'Got to pee.'

As he stepped back from me he started to chuckle. 'Looks like you were telling the truth, you definitely were a virgin.'

Following his gaze I saw a trickle of red running from the countertop where I was perched, down the kitchen cupboard and onto the floor. It took me a few seconds to realize it was my blood.

Bracken smeared a finger into it. 'I'm gonna bottle it,' he said.

'It's disgusting,' I squealed.

'All right, all right. Only joking.' He fetched a dishcloth

from the sink and started very carefully, very tenderly to clean
it up.

'I'm so embarrassed,' I said.

'Don't be,' he smiled his crooked smile. 'That was great,
Becs, honest.'

Upstairs in the bathroom Bracken handed me a scratchy
towel, which I wrapped around my waist while I waited for
the bath to fill. There was a crusty ring round the yellow toilet
bowl and a lone chewed-up toothbrush on the shelf above the
basin.

Bracken was whistling a Jimmy Cliff riff, totally at ease
with being half naked. As he bent down to turn the taps off
I noticed streaks of my blood across the inside of his thighs.

'In you jump,' he instructed, like I was a kid at bath time.
The tub had barely four inches of water in it.

'But there's not enough water.'

'Rubbish.' Bracken hopped in and, instead of lying back
as I always did, knelt and scooped the water up and over
himself to wet and wash his hair.

'Don't you want to put more water in?' I asked.

'Any idea what it costs to heat?' he asked. 'Doesn't grow
on trees, you know.'

When it was my turn, I was too shy to do the kneeling
thing so I put the cold tap on and watched as the fresh water
mingled with the grey of Bracken's leftovers.

He was at the basin now, lathering a bar of soap and
spreading a beard of white bubbles across his face.

'Give us a kiss,' he said and turned round grinning like a
naked Father Christmas.

He came over and kissed me, smearing bubbles all over my face. I screamed and splashed him away, laughing.

When the water had lost every last trace of warmth I got out, wrapped the towel around me and perched on the plastic laundry basket to watch him shave. I'd never seen anyone do it apart from Dad and he used an electric shaver. While Bracken was concentrating in the mirror I ran my fingers round the curve of his bum and down the ridge of muscle on his thigh. He reminded me of the picture of Michelangelo's David that Mum used to keep on her desk.

'Bugger.' Bracken threw the razor in the basin and pointed to a small circle of blood appearing on his cheek.

I stood up and dabbed it gently with my towel.

'Now we're quits,' he said, kissing me, 'I've bled too. Only I made slightly less of a mess.'

Later when we were lying on his bed listening to each other breathing and trying to get our in-and-out breaths in synch, he said, 'Not long till my birthday. You gonna spend it with me?'

'Of course. Will you have a party?'

'Like your neighbour?' His voice was sharp. 'No, thanks very much.' And then more softly, 'Sorry if that disappoints you but there's only one thing I want for my birthday.'

He was lying on his side with his head resting on his hand, staring into my eyes. I'd always thought his eyes were brown but now I noticed there was a ring of green all the way round the edge of the iris. Outside it was just starting to get dark and the birds were calling to each other, making last-minute frenzied dashes to get ready for the night. I didn't notice the noise of the cars any more. It was funny how quickly you got used to things.

'Red,' Bracken whispered urgently. For a moment his face looked like it could collapse, fold in on itself, like a child about to cry. Then in a very quiet voice that was almost like a whine he said my name again.

'What is it?' I suddenly felt scared.

'Red, I love you.'

There was a pause and for that moment it felt like everything had stopped, even our breathing.

'I love you, Becs. Really I do.'

I heard myself reply. I didn't form the words; they just sprang into the gap between us. 'I love you too.'

We lay in silence for a while letting the words settle. For some reason they felt more serious even than having sex for the first time. Like they were some kind of contract or magic spell that once uttered couldn't be broken.

'How old you gonna be anyway?' I don't know why I asked then. It hadn't ever seemed important before. Age was one of those useless facts people were always mistaking for something important. Like wanting to know how many feet Everest was rather than just allowing themselves to marvel at it.

'Guess,' he said.

'Nineteen? Twenty?' I reached up and tickled him under the arm. 'Cradle-snatcher. That's what Sal calls you.'

He shoved my hand away.

'Well, she can sod off. I don't know why you put up with that bitch.'

I turned to face the wall.

'What does it matter anyway?' He traced my spine with his finger. 'We love each other, that's what counts.'

Later, when he was asleep, I crept out of bed and looked in his wallet. I unfolded his creased driving licence. It had his name Stephen J. Bracken and his address but no date of birth as far as I could see, just the year it was valid from. 1963.

I did the calculation. If he'd taken his test as soon as he was allowed he must be twenty-nine.

He was about to turn thirty. In other words he was twice my age. So what? I told myself. Numerical age didn't mean a thing. The world was always trying to reduce stuff that couldn't be understood to mathematical equations. We were soulmates. That's what counted.

Chapter 22

'Was it the ID parade?' asked Marion. 'Is that why you've been off again?'

'How'd you know about it?' Mary-Jane's green eyes drilled into me. The flaky red furrows under them had grown deeper.

'Becs,' said Marion.

'Sorry. Didn't know it was a secret,' I said feebly.

'She was worried about you, that's the only reason she told us,' explained Marion.

Mary-Jane turned to face the window of the school bus. She looked lost hunched there in her navy coat. I was about to move across to sit next to her to try to make things better when Sal bounced up.

'Budge,' she ordered, squeezing in next to Pen so I was wedged against the opposite window by the pair of them.

Phil walked down waving his blue-and-white scarf above his head, chanting, 'Blue is the Colour, Football is the game.'

'Leave it out,' shouted Sal.

'Howsabout about this then,' Dom was trying to sound like Jimmy Saville, 'Trebor mints are a minty bit stronger.'

'Stick 'em up your bum and they last a bit longer,' a chorus of boys' voices sang back.

Pretty soon everyone had joined in.

'He's so daft, my fella,' laughed Sal.

'How come you're not back there with him then?' asked Pen. 'Had a tiff?'

Sal shoved two tightly crossed fingers in Pen's face. 'Don't get funny. Dom and me are like this.'

'What's happening?' Marion hung over the seat in front of us. With her droopy eyes and protruding teeth she looked like one of those dogs with a nodding head that people put on their dashboards.

'I've got something juicy for you all courtesy of Wayne,' said Sal.

'What?' I couldn't help asking even though I'd vowed never to ask Sal anything ever again.

Sal put an arm around Pen. 'Huddle,' she commanded and then whispered, 'The identity parade. Guess who was on it.'

'Pete's dad, I bet,' said Pen.

Marion nodded. 'Got to be. Did you see the calendar in his study at the party?'

'Wrong, not even warm.' Sal drew us closer still. 'It was someone you all know.' She paused, making the most of the moment. 'Someone who's not a million miles away from us right now.'

'Tell us,' pleaded Marion.

'Les,' she said softly. 'Les was on the identity parade.'

'You're not serious, are you?' Pen looked sceptical.

'It doesn't mean anything,' Sal added. 'He was just there. They had to find men of a "certain age" to be on it, so they asked him, he's got grey hair and all.'

'But he'd never lay a finger on anyone. He even drove me home once when I thought I was about to be attacked,' I said.

'Of course he didn't do it,' said Sal. 'Les is pure gold. Anyway, if he'd been the one, Mary-Jane would have recognized him.'

'Then why was he on the parade?' asked Pen.

'I've told you, because they needed blokes on it.'

'It doesn't really make sense, Sal,' said Pen.

'I'm not the one who was saying it was him.' Sal smoothed a loose strand of hair back into her ponytail. 'I'm just telling you what I've been told. Anyway,' she went on, sounding a bit less sure, 'it could just have been someone who looks like Les.'

'Who looks like Les? Come on, girls, spill the beans,' Dom interrupted.

Sal glared at Dom and none of us said anything.

'Keeping secrets from your boyfriend, are you?' said Dom.

'No, it's just, it's none of your business.'

'We'll see about that,' Dom said. He strode to the front of the bus and grabbed Les's *Sun*.

It was only as he sauntered back past us singing 'I've got a lovely pair of coconuts' that I remembered Mary-Jane.

I motioned silently across the aisle to where she was sitting staring out of the window with her back to us.

'I hope she didn't hear,' I whispered to Sal.

'Of course she didn't,' she snapped. 'She's away with the fairies, let's face it.'

Chapter 23

Fenella Jones's mother stood at the bus stop in another maxi, this time an orange kaftan with a headband that resembled a rainbow. As soon as the doors opened she strode purposefully up the steps ignoring Les when he asked if he could help.

'Pass me some sunglasses,' Pen shielded her eyes.

'More like a sick bag,' said Sal.

Through the window I watched Fenella Jones shift from foot to foot. Her white face was splashed with red blotches and in her eyes I recognized the wish to disappear into thin air.

Mrs Jones handed us each an envelope. Her long skirt swished from side to side creating a breeze as she bustled past. 'They are *not* for you,' she said, stressing the 'not' like she was a kindergarten teacher. 'Give these to your parents when you get home this afternoon.'

'PRIVATE AND CONFIDENTIAL' was typed on the envelopes and underneath that 'For Parents Only'.

Sal rushed forward from the back to join us and as soon as Mrs Jones was off the bus we all ripped them open.

Each envelope contained a note on blue paper asking parents to sign the enclosed letter to the County Council 'for all our children's sakes'. The letter itself was typed on plain white paper and addressed to the Chairman of the County Council:

Dear Sir,

I write out of serious concern for the safety of our children to insist that Lesley Robbins be removed immediately from his duties as school bus driver until the identity of the sexual assailant has been established.

Yours faithfully

'Bitch,' pronounced Sal.

'It's a witch hunt,' I said.

'What are we gonna do?' asked Marion.

'This.' Sal stood up on her seat and waved Mrs Jones's letter in the air. 'Come on, you lot,' she yelled, 'all together.'

We climbed onto our seats. When everyone was in position Sal counted to three and then tore the sheets of paper into tiny pieces.

We all copied her, ripping our letters and throwing the shreds as high as we could so that soon the bus was fluttering with blue-and-white paper which looked like confetti and made me think about weddings and about my wedding in particular. I reached for my ring. I'd be the first of our lot to get married. If Bracken allowed me to I'd invite them all. Maybe he'd even let me ask Les.

'I don't understand why she'd do it.' Sarah Slater had left Pete's side to come and discuss it with us. 'Les is the best. Everyone knows that, he'd never hurt a fly.'

'Must have somehow found out about Les and the ID parade,' mused Pen.

'Don't look at me,' said Sal, though we all were because we knew she'd have told Dom, who'd have told everyone.

'Fenella must have told her,' I said.

'Bitch. If Les gets the sack it'll all be because of her,' spat Sal. 'I'm getting Dom involved.'

Not long after, Dom marched to the front and grabbed Fenella Jones's leather briefcase from the overhead rack and hurled it like a rugby ball down to the back. Phil caught it and instead of passing it on he wandered up to Fenella Jones and dangled the bag just above her head.

Everyone laughed as she clawed and flailed until eventually she threw herself at Phil, hitting him with her fists, her frizzy hair a puffball of fury.

'Temper, temper, Bog Brush,' he crowed.

'Here, chuck it here,' ordered Dom and Phil lobbed him the bag in a neat arc.

Fenella Jones retreated to her seat and although we could all hear her crying no one went to comfort her.

'Sit down and shut up,' shouted Les, but he didn't stop the bus like he would have done in the old days.

When the bus arrived at school someone threw Fenella Jones's bag out of the window. As it hit the ground the catch gave way and it flew open so that everything spilt out across the pavement. She scrabbled for her things while all the people who were lining up to leave the bus booed and hissed through the windows at her. When I got off I saw that a little plastic zip-up pouch, the kind you'd keep sanitary towels in, was lying on the curb. I stooped to pick it up for her and then it struck me.

My period.

It hadn't come.

At break-time I headed straight for the loo and checked my knickers. Nothing. Then I got my diary out and checked the dates. I was overdue and my periods were always as regular as clockwork

It's funny how when there's a real crisis your thinking can become crystal clear. At moments of lesser significance you panic, your brain fuzzes over, you can't think straight, you need advice. But when the crisis is really immense there's no panic, there's no fuzziness or drama or confusion to hide behind, there's only the whole of your life whizzing past before your eyes.

That's how it was now. My brain whirred like a precision-made Swiss watch. I had the vision of a soaring eagle or hawk. I could see right to the horizon in every direction of my life.

Outside the cubicle some younger girls were whining about how the whole class had got extra homework just because one person was talking. I wanted to scream at them and tell them they were lucky that's all they had to worry about.

I needed to work out what to do.

For some reason, Mrs Turner's voice came into my head. 'No point crying over spilt milk. What's done is done.'

I needed to be practical.

I ran through my options.

If I told Bracken he might just chuck me. What guy wanted to get saddled with a baby?

If I told Dad he'd kill me.

If I went to the GP he'd have to tell Dad because I wasn't sixteen yet.

If I asked the school for help they'd kick me out like they did Debbie Slater and I wouldn't be able to sit my O levels and then I'd be pregnant without a single qualification to my name.

It was the perfect checkmate.

There was absolutely nothing I could do that wouldn't make it worse. Another of Mrs Turner's phrases came into my head: 'When you're in a hole stop digging.'

I only had one real option and that was to do nothing and hope for the best. Hope that I was wrong and that the whole thing would go away. And if it didn't then I'd deal with it. All I had to do was keep it a secret till August when I was sixteen, then I could run away, or get rid of it or think of something else.

And in the meantime, I'd do what I did when Dad told me Mum had gone. I'd forbid myself from thinking about it.

At home that night I cleared my shelves. I took all the stuffed toys and shoved them in the bottom of my cupboard. Next I took all my idiotic children's books, the *Famous Fives* and the *Secret Sevens* and the *Billy Bunters* and the Ladybird histories, and I pushed them all under my bed so they didn't exist any more.

The only thing I left out from my childhood was the tiny china foal that Mum had put in my stocking the last

Christmas she was here. It was an elegant bay with one white leg. I'd found it wrapped in tissue paper nestled between a bag of chocolate coins and a joke book. At lunch later, when I placed the miniature pony next to me on the table, Mum had leant over, her breath sweet with wine, and whispered that she'd got it because Dad was so mean he wouldn't buy her a real one. Suddenly, in that instant, I'd understood that there was no Father Christmas and that she didn't love Dad any more.

The next day Fenella Jones wasn't on the bus. 'Good riddance to bad rubbish,' said Pen.

'The ID parade didn't even work,' Sal said, picking some dirt out of her nail and wiping it on the seat in front. 'Wayne says he's still out there somewhere.'

'Maybe he's run off with Bog Brush,' giggled Marion.

'Who'd want *her?*' I said and everyone laughed. It was a relief to be with the girls. To be distracted from trying not to think about what might or might not be happening inside my body.

'You should've seen the picture Phil put in her bag,' said Sal. 'A threesome. Two girls and a black guy with his ginormous thing out.'

'Must've been one of Pete's,' Sarah shrugged.

'Serves her right,' I said. 'She could have got Les the sack.'

As we walked into the playground a clumsy-looking girl with falling-down socks was trying to skip in the middle of a giant rope loop. A group of younger girls were chanting, *My mother said, we never should, play with the gypsies in the woods.* We paused to laugh as her oversized Clarks got tangled up in the rope and she hit the ground.

'Flossy knickers,' shouted Sal.

'Mary-Jane used to be brilliant at skipping,' I said.

'She will get better, won't she?' asked Marion.

'Of course,' I replied.

'Come off it,' said Sal.

'My mum thinks she needs to see a head doctor.' Pen's mother was the district nurse, which meant she thought she was God's gift when it came to anything medical.

'More like she needs to eat something,' Sal said and wandered off to give Dom a quick snog.

'Some people do just take things worse than others,' said Pen.

We all nodded like that made sense. But none of it actually made any sense whatsoever. Sometimes it felt like we were no different from flies that at any moment could get crushed by some random act.

Chapter 24

'Don't go near it.' I pushed my canvas school bag under Bracken's bed. 'It's an IRA bomb and it'll kill us both if you touch it.'

Choosing a present for Bracken had been as tricky as trying to find a four-leaf clover. First, I barely had any money as Dad wouldn't let me get a Saturday job like everybody else. Second, I'd wanted to make his first birthday with me perfect, which meant nothing felt right or good enough.

Eventually I'd spotted a pyramid of electric shavers stacked in a corner of Boots. I remembered how he'd cut himself with his old-fashioned razor that first time we'd slept together. If I got him an electric shaver it might mean he'd think of me – of us, together – every time he used it. I didn't have nearly enough money to pay for it so I went home and nicked the rest from Dad's wallet.

We ate dinner in front of the TV. *It's a Knockout* was on. Bracken's mum, Stella, had made us toad-in-the-hole and the three of us ate it with our plates balanced on our knees and our feet resting on the small Formica coffee table.

Stella passed me a bottle of Newcastle Brown. She wore jeans and had short blonde hair that hung in a raggedy flower-pot perm. I'd been terrified of meeting her in case she didn't approve of me and Bracken ended it. But, when I'd looked into her brown eyes and seen they were the same as his, I didn't feel scared any more. Maybe, if I was pregnant, our baby would have eyes that colour too.

'So nice to meet you at last, been hearing a lot about you,' she said, sitting beside me on the sofa.

'Thanks,' I said and then added, 'Thank you so much for having me,' which made me sound stiff and awkward like Dad.

'It's a relief to see him happy at last. Don't mind telling you he's been a bit of a loner over the years.'

On the TV someone was trying to climb a greasy pole while wearing a chicken costume. We all laughed.

'Haven't always lived here.' Stella gestured at the room. 'Had my own kennels when Stephen was born.'

'Going to get you your own place again soon,' said Bracken, passing me another bottle of Newkie Brown. 'Once my business takes off. I want my mum kept in style.'

'He's a good lad.' Stella stretched her legs out and one of the greyhounds rested its head in her lap. 'He'll treat you right. Not like his dad.'

The warm liquid made my head start to spin gently. When I looked over at Stella she'd fallen asleep with a dog sprawling across her feet. Bracken motioned to me and we tiptoed out of the room.

'Do you think she likes me?' I asked once we were in the safety of his bedroom.

'Don't be daft. Of course she does.'

'Do you think I should call you Stephen instead of Bracken when we're here?'

'Red, don't be ridiculous. Stop trying to please everyone.' He shook his head, smiling. 'Just be yourself.' And then he gently lifted off my T-shirt and undid my bra.

In the morning, Stella came into the room with mugs of tea.

'Here you go, dear,' she said as she passed me a mug and then perched at the foot of the bed.

My knickers were lying where they'd fallen in the middle of the carpet. I pulled up the covers and tried to pretend I wasn't totally freaked out. I wondered if Bracken had told her she was going to be my mother-in-law.

'So, do you want your present?' she asked Bracken, like it was completely natural that I was lying there naked in her son's bed.

'Go on then,' he said.

She handed him a box wrapped in paper that had pictures of carol singers and sleighs.

My birthdays hadn't existed since Mum left but when she was still around there'd always be a mountain of parcels, each painstakingly wrapped in different-coloured tissue.

Bracken looked like a small boy as he ripped the paper off. He would've thought I was spoilt if he'd seen how many presents I used to get.

'Thanks, Mum, my favourite,' he said as he pulled out a gift pack of shaving foam and aftershave.

'Loves his Brut,' Stella said to me. 'Never give him anything else.'

'What have you got for me then?' Bracken prodded me.

'Nothing, yet. I was going to buy you something later.' My present was way over the top.

'Liar,' he said. 'You hid it under the bed. Go on, give it me now.' He stuck his bottom lip out like a child having a sulk.

When I didn't move he leant over and reached under the bed. 'Got it.' He waved the present in the air. 'Nice wrapping, eh Mum?'

'Very nice,' she said as Bracken ripped my carefully chosen racing-car paper off, ignoring the card.

'Cool! You shouldn't have, Becs. That looks pricy.' He passed the razor over to his mum to inspect.

'Very nice,' she said, looking at me with an expression that made me want to shrivel up. 'Amazing what money can buy.'

Then she walked out, banging the door as she went.

'Don't mind her,' said Bracken. 'She's just tired.'

But I did mind. I didn't want her to think I was some spoilt girl throwing money around. I wanted her to like me. A wave of fear hit me. I didn't fit in anywhere, that was the truth. Not at home, not at school, not with Sal and the others, and now not even here with Bracken. There was nowhere I belonged. What would happen if I was having a baby? I'd have nowhere to go.

The sun shone through a crack in the curtains above the bed, and a blade of light splashed onto the covers. I should have made Bracken take precautions; I should've said something. If I wasn't so shy, so frightened of putting him off by making a fuss, I wouldn't be in this mess. I held my wrist up into the shard of light, wishing it could slice straight through. Instead it just felt warm and tender.

Bracken took my wrist and started to kiss the skin on the inside of my arm ever so softly. 'I… love…you,' he whispered between kisses as his lips moved slowly up my arm. I didn't want him to see I was starting to cry. I wanted to be invisible. I turned my head away and buried it in the pillow.

'Hey,' he reminded me, 'it's my birthday, aren't I allowed what I want on my birthday?'

I let him turn my head and kiss me and I kissed him back as hard as I could so that he wouldn't notice the tears sliding down my cheeks. I let him run his hands down my body and climb on top of me and I tried not to mind that I just wanted to be cuddled, not have sex.

When it was over he lay back beside me with a big grin. 'Best start to any birthday I can remember.'

'What about your mum, though?'

'Oh for God's sake, come here.' He hugged me tight so that my head was held firmly against his chest. 'She loves you just like I do. Don't give her a second thought.'

'Give me your finger,' I whispered.

He stretched his left hand over and I kissed his little finger where the tip was missing. To start with I'd been freaked out by the uneven, red stump where the section with the nail should've been, but I'd made myself kiss it every time I saw him and now I wasn't scared of it any more.

I lay very still and tried to imagine I was floating on the gentle rise and fall of his breath but deep inside I felt scared. I didn't fit in here. I didn't fit in anywhere and I didn't want to be a mother yet.

Chapter 25

'She's probably making it up,' said Bracken when I tried to explain to him about Les and Fenella Jones and Sal and Mary-Jane. 'She sounds like the kind of girl who wants to be the centre of attention.'

'Who?' I asked. 'Who's making it up? Sal or Mary-Jane?'

'I don't know, either of them, both of them.' Bracken pushed his foot down on the accelerator, making the van rattle. 'Anyway, why do you care so much?'

'I don't care so much,' I said. 'I just can't believe anyone would suspect Les of anything. He's got a wife and a crippled son who'll probably be dead before he's eighteen.'

'You'd be surprised what some guys get up to.'

'I don't want to know.'

'Then stop talking about it. You girls are obsessed.'

'Maybe that's because we're the ones he's after,' I snapped. 'You blokes aren't the ones who've got to live in fear.'

'Calm down, smarty-pants.' Bracken took my hand. His hands were huge compared with mine and had black half-moons of oil under the nails even though he scrubbed them really hard. 'Give us a break. Anyway, I've got a surprise for you. Close your eyes.'

'What, what is it?' I giggled as he took my hand and led me into the garage.

'Okay, open your eyes and hop in.'

Bracken was standing pleased as punch in front of the yellow car that he'd been working on since we'd first met.

'It's finished.' He made a mock trumpeting sound like a fanfare.

I climbed in, disappointed. I'd thought it was going to be a real surprise.

'What do you think of it?'

'What?'

'The Capri.'

'It's all right.'

'It's got a re-con engine with only 4,000 miles on the clock,' said Bracken. 'I'm buying it.'

'What? Why?'

'For us.' He clicked a button on top of the gear stick forward with his thumb. 'It's got overdrive and everything. We don't want to drive about in the van for the rest of our lives.'

'Are you mad?' I'd never raised my voice at Bracken before but I could hear it now sounding loud and crazy.

'I thought you'd be pleased.'

It was as if there was a glass divider in my head that suddenly shattered like a windscreen and all the stuff I'd kept safely stored behind it came spurting out.

'Aren't there a few other things that are more important?' I shouted. 'A few things we need before we get a stupid car?'

'Becs.'

'What about a house of your own, or a job that pays a decent salary, or a bank account that earns interest?' I thought of all the things Dad would want me to have and I screamed them, I screamed them as loud as I could and then I grabbed the door handle.

Bracken took my arm. 'What the hell's going on?'

'It's you,' I shouted. 'You should've been careful.' I yanked at the handle.

'What are you on about?'

'I haven't had my sodding period.'

'You mean you might… you mean you're having a baby?'

'That's not what I said.'

'Seriously, Becs. Are you pregnant?' A giant watermelon grin spread across his face. 'That's the… That's…' He reached across to hug me.

'You're nuts.' I pushed him away. 'I'm fifteen. I can't have a baby when I'm fifteen.'

'Why not?' said Bracken, softly trying to hug me again. 'Mum had me really young.'

'I don't want to hear about your mum. You shouldn't even be living with her at your age. You're an adult.'

I got the door open at last and jumped out of the car. I ran across the cracked concrete forecourt out onto the road. I couldn't be pregnant. All the calmness I'd felt about it had dissolved. It was a disaster. My life was over. I'd destroyed everything in exactly the way they tell you not to. I was a slag. I was totally finished. I hated Bracken. I hated my body. I was a stupid idiot. I'd ruined everything. Dad was right: I was good for nothing. I'd messed up my life before I'd even started it.

I heard Bracken running behind me but I kept going. I cut across the forecourt of one of the low modern buildings and through its empty car park. If I could run fast enough it felt like I might just outpace him and the baby and everything.

I turned down a path between two warehouses and rested for a moment in their shadow where the air felt cool. I needed some time to really think, work things out. But then Bracken was on me, arms around me, trying to make me hug him.

'Don't,' I shouted, 'leave me alone. I can't...'

And then I thought of Debbie Slater working in the Spar forever and of Mary-Jane stuck in her room and I started crying and I cried for them and I cried for me and I cried for all the girls before us and all the ones who would come after and for how hopeless it all was.

'It's okay, Becs, I love you, Becs. We're together.'

But it wasn't okay. I tried to shove him away but then he took my hands and so I kicked at him as hard as I could, but he just dodged his legs out of the way so that I was left kicking into thin air, powerless, pathetic like a fish floundering on a hook. And an image of Fenella Jones trying to grab her bag off Phil sprang into my mind and I thought that I was just as pathetic and hopeless as she was.

Eventually, I started to calm down. 'I'm not having a baby, I'm not.'

'It's okay,' he said without letting go of me. 'You don't have to do anything you don't want to do.'

'You've ruined my life,' I said. I saw him flinch, and knew I'd hurt him.

'Come here.' He let go of my hands and I flung myself against his chest.

He held me and let me cry some more. 'It'll be all right, Becs, I promise. I'm going to take care of you.'

We stood in the shade of the warehouses, like two listing pillars leaning against each other for support. I breathed in deeply, inhaling his familiar smell of oil and dogs and Brut. I let my weight fall harder against him and felt how he was solid, he didn't budge, not an inch. I turned my head so my face rested against his shoulder. There was something about leaning on him like that that felt so safe.

'Red,' he whispered, stroking my hair, 'you don't need to be scared. I'll take good care of you.'

He hadn't let me run away. Even though I'd shouted those horrible things, he'd come after me. He didn't end it like I'd thought he would. He even wanted the baby. He wanted me. He wanted it all to work.

I thought of the falcon nesting on the water tower and how he'd helped her look after her chicks, how he always looked out for his mum. He was a good man, a man I could trust.

Maybe I could have his baby after all.

Maybe I wasn't ruining my life.

Maybe the baby would be adorable.

Maybe it would look like him.

Maybe Dad would come round in the end.

Maybe he'd want me to name him Cecil after him and have a proper christening with a frilly white frock.

And if Dad didn't come round?

It would be okay. I'd have my own family.

We'd get on fine.

Bracken, me and our son. (Because it would be a boy. I knew it.)

I used Bracken's T-shirt to wipe the tears and snot off my face and let him lead me back to the road. He put his arm round me. 'That's my girl. You don't need to worry about a thing.'

Although it must've been past five, the sun still felt warm on my skin as we passed out of the shadow of the buildings. I must have looked a sight with my eyes all red and mucous smeared in all directions.

As we crossed the road back towards the garage, a white bird flitted from nowhere across the cloudless sky and landed right in front of us on the roof of Bracken's van.

'Looks like a dove,' said Bracken. 'Like in Noah's ark. A sign.'

He went into the garage and came back out carrying a tin of birdseed.

'Ground's too hard for them to get the worms out,' he explained and offered me a handful to scatter. The bird flew down and started pecking at the seeds. Before long starlings and tits and blackbirds had joined in.

'Come on, Becs, let's get you back before your Dad's home,' he said, shutting the garage door. 'I don't want you getting into trouble, especially not now in your condition.'

Chapter 26

Stella pointed to a cardboard box of clothes sitting amongst the jumble of shoes in the hallway. 'You're going to have my room, I've started shifting stuff out already. It won't be as nice as what you're used to, I'm sure, but it'll give you more space at least.'

I glared at Bracken. He'd promised he wouldn't tell anyone. He blew me a kiss and then wrapped his arms around Stella.

'And Mum's going to take care of the baby so you can stay at school and do A levels if you want to, aren't you, Mum?'

'We're not having you ruining your education like I did,' Stella replied, pushing Bracken away. 'Now you two go and watch some telly while I put the tea on. Got you a nice steak, Becs, to keep you strong.'

I followed Stella into the kitchen. 'What can I do to help?'

'Not a thing,' she smiled. 'Just keep making my son happy.'

*

Later, as I lay on Bracken's bed he examined my tummy as if he was a doctor, then he lay his head flat against it, listening.

'Nothing.' He kissed my belly button before circling it with his tongue. 'Flat as a pancake. How do we know that it's really there?'

'It's too little to see, like a bulb under the ground.' I acted like I knew, but secretly I kept looking at it too, wondering when a bump would appear. I hung onto the fact that I felt just a teeny bit sick each morning. Not enough to stop me doing anything but just enough to help me believe it was real.

Bracken started drumming his fingers on my tummy.

'What are you doing?'

'Morse code. I'm trying to tell it we love it.'

Downstairs the drone of the hoover started. I felt a sudden wave of irritation. 'Did you have to tell your mum already?'

'I'm sorry. I just knew how chuffed she'd be. She's gonna help you. You'll see it's all going to be all right.'

'I could just get rid of it.'

'What?'

'Once I'm sixteen, go to a clinic, you know.' I sat up and scooped my hair into a ponytail.

Bracken sat up beside me, furious. 'You what? You're saying you'd actually think about killing our baby?'

'I didn't mean that.'

'Haven't you listened to a fucking word I've said?' he shouted.

'Bracken, don't.'

'What about me haven't you understood?' He put his face up close to mine and then shoved me back flat onto the bed.

His voice was loud enough and angry enough for his mum and all the neighbours to hear. He leant over me, pinning me down beneath him. 'Which bit of you would think it was okay to kill our baby?'

I started crying.

His face softened. 'Promise me, Becs. Promise me. I want you to promise now, right now, that you'll never ever hurt our baby. Got it?'

I nodded.

'Promise,' I said. 'Promise.'

'Promise,' I sobbed. 'I give my word.'

He lay back down beside me, calm again. His temper was like a storm. It blew up out of nowhere and then suddenly it was gone.

'Sorry. Didn't mean to lose my cool. I just couldn't deal with it if anything happened.'

One of my shoulders throbbed from where he'd held me down. He stroked my forehead, gently brushing wisps of hair off my face. 'I'd be finished if anything happened to the baby. If anything went wrong between us.'

'I just don't want you to feel like, you know, like you're trapped or anything.' I wiped my eyes on his T-shirt.

'Don't be an idiot,' he smiled. 'There's nothing I want more.'

He held me for a minute and then he lifted up my shirt. 'Now, what about these?' He ran a finger round the curve of each of my breasts. 'Any change here?'

And then before I knew it he was kissing them in turn. I buried my fingers in his thick dark hair and cradled his head as he sucked and pulled at my nipples.

'Just a sec.' Bracken pulled away and got up to put on an album. Other people used dope or LSD. Bracken had music.

'Do you think it's all right?' he paused, just before he went inside me. 'Do you think I'll hurt the baby?'

'No,' I replied, though really I wasn't sure.

He was extra careful anyway. Really slow and gentle, just going a little way inside of me and then out. He held himself up on his arms and looked down at me lying beneath him. David Bowie was singing,

> *Oh you pretty things*
> *Don't you know you're driving your*
> *Mamas and Papas insane*

Bracken's top lip curled into his funny-shaped smile. 'Pretty thing,' he whispered. 'That's what you are. You're my pretty thing.' Then he closed his eyes and started to move in and out more quickly.

I closed my eyes too and tried to give in to the rhythm. It still hurt a bit but I didn't care. I tilted my hips upwards.

'Don't,' he moaned and then his body shuddered and it was over and he was lying on top of me, taking most of his weight on his elbows so he didn't squash me and I could feel his sweat gluing us together.

'Shall I keep going?' he asked. 'For you?'

'No,' I whispered. 'It was perfect.'

The headlights of the passing cars flashed across the room like searchlights. On the floor by the chest of drawers I could see Bracken's neat pile of folded clothes. I rested my hand on my tummy and tried to imagine our tiny, invisible baby floating inside me. And I felt glad. When I didn't think about Dad or school it was all fine.

'Almost forgot to tell you,' Bracken beamed. 'Our money worries are over. Going to be able to keep you like a lady.'

'What are you on about?' I hated it when he spoke about me like I needed to be spoilt. He and Stella both did it.

'Yours truly got himself a new job. Special deliveries,' he announced proudly. 'Bloke came into the garage, got chatting and he offered it to me on the spot.'

'Congratulations,' I said, taking his left hand and kissing his little finger.

'I'll still have the garage. All I've got to do is drive to Coventry twice a week. Tuesdays and Thursdays. I'll earn more from each trip than I make in a week mending cars. Told you fate was on our side.'

I leant over and kissed him and then stretched above his head to touch the wooden window frame. 'Don't tempt fate,' I told him. 'Touch some wood.'

'Don't be daft,' he said. 'The gods love us. You've got to learn to trust, Becs. Not everything turns out bad.'

Chapter 27

I waited inside the corner shop behind the magazine rack, so nobody would spot me and ask awkward questions. There was no way I was going to miss Bracken's first trip to Coventry.

Mr Rahman who owned the shop looked at me suspiciously and said, 'No school this afternoon?'

'Waiting for my dad,' I replied. 'Doctor's appointment.'

He shrugged and went back to pricing up some Topics. I bought a bag of salt and vinegar Chipsticks so he wouldn't think I was taking the mickey and ate them slowly, trying to get as many nibbles out of each one as I could. Sal had the record. She once got fifty-six out of one Chipstick. The most I'd ever got was thirty-two.

When I saw Bracken's van through the shop window I rushed out and climbed straight into the cab.

'Quick,' I said like he was a getaway driver.

With tyres squealing we sped through town with Bracken beating everyone off the mark at the lights.

'This is a lot more fun than double Chemistry.'

'Exactly,' said Bracken. 'Why do you think I left school?'

Bracken was the only person I knew who'd actually dropped out. The second he turned fifteen he just left and started work. Nobody even bothered to try to make him come back.

'Learnt more from listening to music and real life than I ever did from a beak.'

It had never occurred to me before that not staying at school was even an option. I'd always just assumed I'd do what Mum and Dad did, take my exams and go to university. Now, though, sitting in Bracken's cab with a warm breeze skimming across my skin and the radio playing full blast I understood that there was a whole other world out there.

The Grateful Dead came on with a song about hitching across America.

I slipped my shoes off and put my bare feet on the dashboard. Then I wrapped my school tie round my head. Bracken already looked like he was on his way to Woodstock with his shades and faded denim and shaggy hair. He was a mass of contradictions. Although he looked like a hippy he was one hundred per cent reliable. He was always where he said he'd be, took care of his mum and now he was going to take care of me.

When the chorus began we both joined in. *Freedom's just another word for 'nothing left to lose'.*

I started laughing. I suddenly got it. This flash of wisdom cracked across my mind as bright as lightning across a midnight sky.

I'd spent my childhood thinking grown-ups knew what was best but actually they hadn't got a clue. Dad had spent his life obeying rules and conventions that he'd inherited without thinking and look where it'd got him. He was a sad, lonely old man. He had no idea what happiness was. He thought it was what you got by doing what was expected, by accumulating qualifications and possessions. That wasn't happiness – that was oppression. There was no way I wanted to be like him.

Maybe it was being pregnant that made me see things so clearly. I'd never before seen how pointless everything I'd been told to work for was. Sitting in this van, singing, with a man I loved beside me, I had everything I needed. Who could want anything more? Who needed exam certificates when I had it all right here, right now? I was free.

'Shall we go through the city centre? Have a butcher's?' asked Bracken when we got to Cambridge.

I nodded. I'd been here once when Dad and Mum wanted to show me where they'd met. Mum said she'd fallen for Dad because he'd seemed so solid and sensible.

Then the city had seemed magical, full of spires and old sandstone buildings. Looking at it now, it seemed artificial, out of touch, a page from an ancient story, just like Mum and Dad's great romance.

'This is where Dad wants me to go. Can you believe it? This is what he thinks is going to make me happy.'

'And would it?' asked Bracken.

'You're what makes me happy,' I said. 'Dad only wants me to come here so he can boast to his colleagues. It's not about me.'

Bracken reached over and took my hand. 'I don't mind,' he said. 'If you do want to come here we can get somewhere to live and you can be a student and I'll find a garage and look after the baby and…'

'Shut up,' I protested. 'I don't want it. Why would I want to come to a place like this and be surrounded by posh idiots like I met at Pete's party?'

'Because you're smart?' Bracken glanced at me quizzically. 'I want my baby to have a happy mum.'

'I am happy, I'm with you.'

'And with our baby.' Bracken gave my tummy a gentle pat.

As we drove out the other side of town and the buildings became normal and unpretentious and suburban again, I took Bracken's hand and kissed his stumpy finger and then rested his palm across my heart.

'I want you to understand. Really understand. I don't want anything else. This is enough.'

I'd never been on a motorway before. Dad and I never went anywhere, so why would I have been? It felt exciting as we joined the stream of cars hurtling up the M1 like I was crossing yet another new frontier.

'This is where we could do with a decent motor,' Bracken complained. 'It's bloody shit. Can't get more than sixty-five out of it.'

'Aren't we going fast enough? It sounds like we're about to explode.'

'We'd be doing a ton by now if we had that Capri.' Bracken pushed the accelerator pedal against the floor.

'You see, you're not happy with what you've got. You want more.'

'Becs, I'm a bloke. Of course I want a faster car.'

'What happens if you want a faster, better me?' I asked. 'Are you going to trade me in one day for a better model?'

'Don't be ridiculous.'

'It's not ridiculous. Pete's dad left his mum for a younger woman and now his mum has nobody to spend Christmas with.'

'You and your stories, Becs. I'm not like that.' He ran a hand through his hair. 'I'm with you for life just like it says on my tattoo.'

The radio started crackling. I twisted the knob but all the stations had turned to static so I found an Eagles tape in the glove compartment and shoved it in. Outside the world was rushing by, cars whipped past us with just inches to spare. We overtook lorries with huge trailers that looked like they could topple over and crush us if the wind blew too hard. We were one part of a massive speeding, snaking string of metal boxes hurtling in the same direction down a strip of concrete through the middle of the English countryside. Signs with names of places I'd never heard of flashed by. I was seeing more than I'd ever learnt in a Geography class.

'What would happen if we crashed now?' I asked. 'You know, just hit the car in front or the safety barrier?'

'Curtains,' he said.

'If I died now, I'd die so happy.'

I wished I could prove to him how much I loved him. I thought about the end of *Tess of the D'Urbervilles* when she's finally content and with Angel. When the police come to take her away and hang her she's almost glad because the happiness was so much she knew it could never have lasted. That's how I felt. I didn't want it ever to end or be less perfect than it was now.

I reached across and put a hand on the steering wheel. I let it rest for a moment and then I pulled at the wheel. The van veered into the next lane. A car honked a loud long angry honk.

'Becs, for fuck's sake. What're you doing?'

'Sorry.' I let go of the wheel.

'What's going on? You could have killed us.'

I started to cry.

'Fucking hell, Becs.'

'Sorry, I just can't believe it's possible to be this happy. I don't ever want it to end, I want it to feel like this forever, for eternity.'

'It's not going to ever end,' said Bracken.

'Of course it will.'

'Bullshit, Becs.'

'Even if you don't leave me, what about when one of us dies?'

Bracken gave me a triumphant crooked grin. 'Then whoever goes first just waits in heaven. Simple. Now how about you getting some kip? Can't have you getting overtired.'

I put my hand on top of his.

'Just do us one favour, Becs?'

'What?'

'Next time you're happy, just tell me with words. Don't try to kill us both. Eh? I wanna live, have this baby. Live happily ever after.'

'Me too,' I smiled.

I leant back and closed my eyes and let the rumbling of the tyres and the shaking of the van lull me to sleep.

Chapter 28

When I woke up we were in Coventry. It was cold and the sky had turned steel grey. We were barely moving and the crawling line of cars in front of us stretched as far as I could see.

'It's sodding rush hour,' Bracken said. He had a map spread out across the steering wheel, which he was trying to read while he was driving. 'There are no effing streets marked on it.'

'Do you want me to have a look?'

'I just told you,' he snapped, 'there's no names marked on it.'

We sat in silence as the traffic inched along. Bracken ripped the map down the middle and then scrunched each half into two balls, which he threw as hard as he could out of the window. The second one bounced off the bonnet of a car going in the opposite direction and the driver rolled down his window and stuck two fingers up at us. Bracken waved his fist back.

'Shall we ask someone?'

'Becs. Just leave it out.'

I turned away and rolled down the window.

Eventually Bracken had to ask for directions but it turned out there were quite a few streets with the same name and we didn't know which area the one we wanted was in so we had to try them all. By the time we got to the right one it was nearly dark.

'I hope he's still here.' Bracken spat on each of his hands and tried to smooth down his hair. 'Red, I didn't mean to get narky. Just don't want to mess up this chance.'

I tried to smile as he gave me a peck on the lips.

'Wait here. I'll be back in a sec.' He reached across into the glove compartment and took out an envelope.

'Aren't I coming too?'

'Not really the kind of place for you.' He slammed the door and was gone before I could protest.

The Kings Head had metal grilles on the windows and no tubs of welcoming red geraniums like you'd get in the country. The car park was empty except for another van parked almost exactly opposite. A guy sat in it smoking. I watched the tip of his cigarette glow larger each time he took a drag. It looked like he was staring at me.

I pressed the lock down on both doors and wondered whether he'd be able to smash the window in if he tried. Even if he just came over and tried the door or pressed his face up against the windscreen it would scare me so much that the shock could hurt the baby. I stared at the pub door willing Bracken to hurry up and come out before it was too late.

Bracken didn't come. I wondered whether I should go into the pub and try to find him but then that might ruin everything, so instead I rummaged around to try to find something to defend myself with. In the back behind Bracken's seat I found a large metal spanner and grabbed it just in case. I sat there holding it with both hands. For some reason Pete came into my mind. What would Pete Mantoni think if he saw me now sitting here waiting for his father's mechanic, in fact what would any of the others think? Who cares? I told myself and tried to recite 'The Owl and the Pussycat', which Mum always used to read to me, only I couldn't remember the words.

When Bracken finally appeared his breath stank of booze.

'Sorry about that. Had to buy the bloke a pint or two to make up for keeping him waiting.'

'I could've been attacked or raped while you were in there.'

'What?'

'There was this dead creepy guy watching me.'

'Where?' Bracken opened the door ready to jump out.

'He's gone, it wasn't a big deal, really.'

'I'm sorry, Becs. I should never have brought you with me.'

We wove back through tiny streets and onto the main road until we were back following signs for the M1. It was only then that I noticed the time. Dad was going to go crazy.

Bracken stopped at a phone box and gave me some change but when I heard Dad's voice and the pips my mind went blank, I couldn't think what to say so I just hung up.

'I'll speak to him,' said Bracken.

I shook my head. I couldn't face telling him that Dad still didn't know he existed.

Bracken ran his hand up my bare leg. 'I wish you'd let me do it right. I want to ask him for your hand in marriage. He'd come round if he met me.'

'Don't even think about it. He'd kill me. He spends his life putting people in jail. We've got to wait till we're already married and it's too late for him to stop us.'

'All right. Keep your hair on. It was only a suggestion.'

We passed a row of shops and Bracken pulled over again.

'Wait here,' he said. 'Promise I'll only be a minute this time.'

When he came out of the shop he had a carrier bag in his hand.

'We're going to celebrate,' he said, revealing a four-pack of Babycham. 'These trips'll pay for our wedding and a down payment on a flat.'

The bottles rattled and clinked on my lap as we headed for the motorway. After five minutes, when we were almost out of the city, Bracken pulled into a lay-by next to a sports field. Grabbing the bag he went round to the back of the van. I was feeling more and more tense about Dad and how mad he was going to be when I finally got home.

'Hurry up,' I pleaded.

'Come round here,' he shouted.

'We've got to go.'

'Just for a minute, Becs, I promise.'

I walked round to the back. Bracken had both the doors open and had laid out a blanket inside the van and put the Babycham in the middle of it, like it was a picnic or something.

'After you,' he said, offering me his arm, so I put my foot on the tow bar and climbed into the back.

'Cheers.' He handed me a bottle.

'What about the baby? I don't think I should.'

'It's as weak as gnat's piss this stuff. Bottoms up.' He held out his bottle and clinked it against mine.

We sat with our backs against the cold metal side of the van and drank the Babycham. I tried to relax but I couldn't. Dad was going to freak out so badly. Bracken had left the engine running so we could have music. Dylan was singing 'Lay Lady Lay'. I closed my eyes and tried to drift away on his words. *Why wait any longer for the one you love, when he's standing in front of you?*

The next thing I knew Bracken was on me, kissing me and trying to get me to lie back flat on the blanket. I didn't want to. I was too worried about Dad and home and the time.

But I didn't want to hurt Bracken's feelings and so I gave in and let him lie me down and climb on top of me. Once he was inside me I dug my fingers into his back and groaned. Bracken always said it was a real turn-on if I made a noise and sounded like I was enjoying it. My head banged against the metal floor as he pushed himself as far inside me as he could. I groaned some more and he came.

'Sounds like somebody had a good time,' Bracken winked at me as he zipped himself back into his jeans.

Chapter 29

I tried to slide past the door of the study and up the stairs to my room but Dad heard me.

'No you don't. In here, now.'

He pointed to the hard-backed chair opposite his desk where he made Mrs Turner sit when he was giving her lists of what he wanted her to do.

'I demand an explanation.' On the wall above his head a row of dead butterflies stared out from their glass tomb. They'd always given me the creeps, delicate little creatures pinned wide open so he could admire them.

When I remained silent Dad drained his glass and refilled it from the crystal decanter.

'I'm not going to stand by and watch you destroy your future.'

His desk was crowded with documents, some still in neat bundles tied with pink ribbons, others opened and seemingly strewn at random.

'Rebecca, I will not have you out at all hours. I will not be disrespected in this way. Do you understand?'

Through the open door into the hallway I spotted our coats hanging neatly in a line. Beneath them, in the metal stand amongst Dad's umbrellas, I could see my tennis racket poking out.

'A floozy. That's what you're becoming, do you understand? A common, good-for-nothing floozy. You might as well go and live with Mrs Turner on her council estate. You are ruining yourself. Understand?'

I got up and walked out of the study.

'Come back,' I heard Dad command as I slammed the door.

'I'm not surprised Mum left you,' I muttered back.

I tugged my green army surplus rucksack out from under my bed and started to pack. A handful of knickers, two bras, my jeans, a couple of T-shirts and my purple Southern Comfort sweatshirt. From the shelves above my bed I plucked my complete works of Shakespeare, *Tess of the D'Urbervilles* and the tiny china foal Mum gave me. I'd take my sandals and my gym shoes and that was all. There was no way I was going to wait till I was sixteen to start my life with Bracken. I was going now.

Doing up the buckles on the bag I realized I'd forgotten to pack a nightie. I'd need one if I was going to be bumping into Stella when I went to the loo in the night. Mrs Turner always ironed my nighties and left them folded in my pine cupboard. Dad made her iron everything. It was a total waste of time.

Inside the wardrobe my white school shirts hung neatly in a row and for some reason the sight of them stole all the wind from my sails. I stared at the shirts, five of them, one for each day. My uniform. I'd nearly forgotten.

Carefully, I folded each of them, one arm at a time, and slid them gently into the rucksack. It was only as I did this that I began to wonder how I was going to carry on at school if I'd run away from home. Dad would tell the school and then when I showed up for lessons they'd call him or have me arrested or something awful and humiliating like that. It was pointless taking my uniform with me. If I left home I'd have to quit school too.

I stared out of the window into the night sky. I wished Mum was here. When I allowed myself to think of her I always imagined she was walking barefoot on a beach some-where, laughing her beautiful laugh while the thin gold bangles she always wore tinkled happily on her wrist. The older I got the easier it was for me to understand why she went. She didn't have a choice. She'd met someone she could really love.

Mrs Turner told me later that after she'd gone Dad drove himself crazy trying to find her. He'd rung everyone who knew her, then he'd called the police and when they couldn't help he'd finally hired private detectives. There was no trace.

'My guess is she went overseas,' Mrs Turner told me. 'A free spirit your mother was.'

A free spirit sounded cool.

I only had one memory of the night she left and it was hazy so I was never quite sure it was real. I was lying in bed and she sat beside me smelling of Chanel No. 19 as usual. She'd rested her elegant hand on my forehead as if I might have a fever and then she'd leant over and whispered very softly that she'd come back and get me, as soon as she could.

My rucksack lay open on the floor and I suddenly felt very tired. What would happen if Mum did come back and I wasn't here? And what would happen to Dad if he was left all alone? He'd never survive. I couldn't leave him right now. I took my jeans off and put my nightie on. Maybe it was a cop-out or maybe I was just too exhausted but it felt like I should stay put for now, just till I'd got my exams out of the way and then I could start my new life with Bracken.

Chapter 30

Weird. I could have sworn I'd heard Dad in the kitchen. He should've been on his way to London on the 6.42 or whatever stupid train it was he caught. I peeked through the swing door and sure enough there he was sitting at the table with a cup of coffee in front of him and his suit jacket on the back of the chair. I decided to act normal and breezy like nothing had happened.

'Morning, Dad.' I was casual as anything. 'Lost your job?'

His mouth didn't even flicker towards a smile.

'Sit down.'

He probably had a monumental hangover. If I was lucky he wouldn't even be able to remember that last night's row had happened.

'Sorry, I can't, Dad. I'll miss the bus. Don't want to be late for school.' I made myself plant a kiss on the top of his bald head as I made for the back door.

'Not so fast, young lady. I said sit down.'

'Do you have to have a go at me this early in the morning?'

'Rebecca.'

I took a seat across the kitchen table from him.

'What about school?' I said. 'I don't want a late mark.'

'Rebecca, I don't think you understand the severity of your situation. This is your O-level year.'

Not again. I tipped my chair back. There was a blackbird on the washing line outside. Sometimes Bracken and I would be driving along and he'd point to what looked like an empty sky and then out of it would soar a bird that I hadn't even been able to see and he'd know exactly what type it was and what it ate and whether it migrated.

'Look at me while I'm speaking to you.'

I stared back at him and tried to make him disappear. In RE Mr Speckles said Jesus could walk on water because he believed he could. The mind has incredible powers.

'We're going back to basics. This is Year Zero.'

'What are you talking about, Dad? I need to go to school.'

'Where were you yesterday?'

I shrugged.

'Where were you?'

I slipped Bracken's ring off my finger and put it into my pocket. 'What about my right to silence, Dad? I thought you believed in human rights.'

Dad sighed. 'You leave me no choice, Rebecca. As I can't trust you to be left alone from now on you'll be taken to school by Mrs Turner and collected by Mrs O'Dwyer.'

'Mrs O'Dwyer? You've got to be joking. I'll be a laughing stock.'

'I fail to see what anyone would find funny about Mrs O'Dwyer. She has also kindly agreed to supervise your revision, which she will do until you've sat and completed your examinations. We're fortunate she lives so close.'

'Dad, you're overreacting.'

'You've left me no option.'

'What if I promise never to be late home again?'

'It's too late, Rebecca.'

'Why, Dad? Please, just one more chance.'

There was nothing I could do. Dad was adamant and kept going on about 'Year Zero' and how even the phone was going to be locked. I told him that Year Zero was invented by Pol Pot who was an evil mass murderer, who killed his own people for being intelligent or wearing glasses, not a loving parent.

'We're starting from scratch,' Dad said. 'You have no freedom until you've shown me you deserve it.'

Chapter 31

'You're jammy, getting chauffeured to and from school.' Sal prodded me like it was funny and then picked up a plate of chips and handed over her dinner ticket.

'It's a disaster. How am I ever going to see Bracken if I'm handcuffed to Mrs OD? He's going to think I've stood him up. Can you give him something for me so he'll know why I can't make it?' I reached into my pocket and pulled out a note I'd written him in break. I put my hand out to give it to her.

'For God's sake. Can't you think about anything else?' Sal ignored the note and glanced over to Dom who was already sitting down with a bunch of the others.

'Sal, that's not fair. You see Dom every single day. Before school, after school, during school.'

'That's 'cos Dom's not some dirty old man,' she sneered. 'Anyway, it'll do you good to have some time apart, might bring you to your senses.'

Then off she flounced to Dom wiggling her bum like she was God's gift.

'Cow! Selfish cow!' I shouted after her but the din of the canteen swallowed my words up. I shoved the bit of paper back in my pocket.

I stood for a moment surrounded by people chatting and elbowing and clinking chipped glasses. The stench of gammon and semolina made me want to gag. Pen had just joined the back of the line. I could ask her but she was too sensible. She could tell someone. Then I spotted Marion a bit further up the line. She had her socks round her ankles as usual and was looking around like she was lost.

'Pongs today, doesn't it?' I said, joining her in the queue.

'Takes forever as well.' Marion saw Sal sitting down and waved frantically to her.

'Can I ask you a favour?' I yanked at the bottom of my shirt, which I'd started to wear untucked in case I'd started to look fatter without knowing it. I checked to make sure no teachers were nearby. 'Could you give Bracken this?'

'What?' Marion screwed up her face.

'Could you give this to Bracken?' I shoved the piece of paper into her hand. 'Please, Marion, it's really, really important.'

She looked at the folded paper, which I'd taped round the edges.

'It's private,' I said.

Marion glanced over towards Sal again. 'How am I meant to get it to him?'

'Just go up to him after school, he'll be at the gate waiting for me. Just give it to him and tell him it's from me.'

'What if someone sees me?'

'It's not a crime.'

Marion picked up a tray as we were nearly at the front of the queue.

'Please.' I took her arm. 'Come on, I'll get your lunch.' I handed the dinner lady my meal ticket.

She put her dinner ticket back in her red patent purse and then squeezed my note in beside it. 'You'll have to say you made me do it if I get caught.'

'Thanks, Marion. You're a real friend.'

She loaded her tray with ham and chips and stewed apple and custard and trotted off to sit with the others.

After school, Mrs OD made me wait outside the lab while she got ready. Everyone walked past me standing there like an idiot. It was humiliating, like I was back in kindergarten. A small ladybird landed on my arm. I flicked it off and then felt guilty when it lay sprawling on the concrete.

Mrs OD was taking forever. I could see her through the window wiping the board, tidying her desk, stacking piles of homework. I could just make a run for it – leg it across the playground, through the gate to Bracken. I'd jump in the van and we'd drive. We'd drive somewhere far away, somewhere Dad would never find me. We could have the baby and nobody would know I was meant to be at school, we'd lie about my age, we could have a life together. No one would call him a cradle-snatcher or say mean things. We'd just be a normal couple.

'Ready?' Mrs O'Dwyer stood beside me. 'I'm in the car park.'

She strode off, away from the main gate towards the playing field where the staff left their cars, her large tweed skirt swaying. I had a split second to make a decision – go with her or run away. My heart wanted me to break free but I didn't. I *couldn't*. I couldn't risk Dad finding out yet. If I disappeared he'd hire detectives or call the police like he did with Mum and they'd blame Bracken because I was underage.

Mrs O'Dwyer let me sit in the front of her Hillman Imp, which reeked of the same chemicals as her lab. The flesh of her knobbly feet bulged through her sensible sandals as she changed gear. I rolled down the window to try to escape the smell.

Bracken must have read my note by now. I hoped he wasn't too pissed off. He'd probably have gone back to the garage. I wondered what Marion thought of him. I bet she'd got an instant crush and had told Sal how he was a million times dishier than Dom. I wondered how many days it would be till I could be with him again.

At the main gate I instinctively looked to where Bracken always waited and jumped when I saw his white van was there glinting in the sun. The doors were open and Bracken was leaning against it, in his denim jacket and shades, watching for me. Mrs O'Dwyer craned her neck to see whether it was safe to pull out, and that's when he saw me.

'Hey, Becs,' he shouted. 'What are you doing?'

'Who's that?' snapped Mrs O'Dwyer, as she pulled out onto the road.

'Hey, where are you going?' Bracken shouted.

I wanted to answer. I wanted to lean out of the window and shout but I didn't dare. I just sat stock still like a statue, staring straight ahead through the windscreen like I hadn't

seen him, like he didn't exist. I couldn't afford to be impetu-
ous or Dad would find out. I had to think strategically. One
false move and it'd be like Romeo and Juliet; except we
wouldn't actually be dead, we'd just be trapped for good in a
life without each other, which amounted to the same thing.

As soon as we rounded the corner I knew I'd made the
wrong decision.

I was an idiot. How could I just have ignored him? I'd
jump out at the next junction and run back to find him and
then everything would be all right. Almost as if she could read
my mind Mrs OD reached across me and flicked down the
lock on my door.

'Can't be too careful. I didn't like the look of that man,
Rebecca. How would someone like that know your name?'

Chapter 32

I couldn't sleep that night. I couldn't sleep all weekend.

Dad didn't let me out of the house.

In my mind's eye I kept seeing Bracken calling to me. I kept seeing myself ignore him.

I was no better than Judas (or was it Peter?) who said he'd never seen Jesus before. What was love if you didn't put it into action, if you were a coward and tried to calculate everything in your head instead of just acting when you had the chance?

I got out the Bible I'd been given for Confirmation. It was Peter who'd ignored Christ. Basically the Crucifixion never would have happened if Peter hadn't denied Jesus. That's what I did to Bracken. I denied him.

A crime of omission, Dad would have called it. I looked that up too: a criminal failure to act.

Hamlet failed to act and look what happened. Everyone died.

Not acting was what finished Mum and Dad off too.

If Dad had told Mum he loved her she never would have had to leave him for someone else who did.

I gathered my essentials and hid them inside my gym bag. The weekend crawled past. I spent it in my room to avoid Dad.

On Sunday night I wrote a note and left it under my pillow. As I placed it there I wondered whether it was Mum or Dad who'd played the part of tooth fairy, slipping a coin onto the same place where now I was leaving the note.

It's not that I don't love you, I wrote, it's just that I need to find Mum so I've gone to America to be with her.

Of course, I didn't know that she was in America. But I needed to say somewhere far away. I wanted him to think I'd gone to the airport to catch a plane. I figured it would buy me and Bracken enough time to get away somewhere safe and lie low until we could get married. Dad might even wind up being glad that Bracken had made an honest woman of me, that I'd chosen someone honourable.

Chapter 33

On Monday the weather turned. It was the first day of rain for weeks and rather than a gentle spring rain, it was a huge great grey heaving biblical rain, the same kind that must have sent Noah scurrying to build his ark. I didn't have a coat, just the nightie, knickers and socks I'd shoved in with my PE kit. It hadn't occurred to me to pack a coat or even a jumper. Somehow when the sun was shining it was hard to imagine it ever raining again.

By the time I got to the gate my shirt was so sodden that the pink rosebuds on my bra were showing through. Sal had taken the piss out of my underwear after netball, said it was babyish. Her bras were always lacy and underwired but then she didn't have to rely on Mrs Turner to buy them. I didn't tell her that Bracken loved this bra, that he'd gently kissed my nipples through the cotton until they went hard and told me my tits were perfect.

I had to move quickly so Mrs OD didn't catch me.

'Where are you off to in such a hurry? I thought you were under lock and key?' asked Pen as I raced past her.

'Got a day off for good behaviour.'

'So you can come home on the bus with us?'

'Actually I'm going to meet Bracken.'

'Your funeral,' said Pen and peeled off to where Sal and Marion and Sarah Slater were huddled under a tree.

A small flood of water had formed on the pavement outside the gate. A twerp of a boy was stamping in it trying to splash any girls coming out. I tiptoed through in my sandals, trying to look ladylike in case Bracken was watching.

I slipped my engagement ring onto my finger. I didn't need to hide it any more. For some reason I suddenly felt stupidly shy about seeing Bracken and telling him I was leaving home and coming to him at last, just like he'd wanted.

All around me kids were running and shrieking and laughing. Some of them had got their school bags on their heads, a few mums had brought brollies, but mostly people were just getting soaked. I could feel the rain dripping from the ends of my hair down my back but Bracken wouldn't mind how I looked. He was always just happy to see me.

Only, Bracken wasn't there.

I stood in the middle of the pavement and stared at the empty space where I thought he'd be waiting. Then I looked up and down the street.

It hadn't occurred to me that he wouldn't be there. He was always there.

Any minute now the others would come out to catch the bus. I didn't want them to see me standing like an idiot in the rain and know that Bracken hadn't come. I didn't want them trooping past me, asking questions. I didn't want them to see me crying. So I started walking as if everything was fine, as if I had somewhere important to go.

I walked up to the main road and then turned towards the town centre, the way Bracken always did. I kept my eyes peeled on the road, willing his white van to come whizzing past. Maybe he was late. Maybe a customer had come into the garage at the last minute. I walked up towards the station past the fish and chip shop. He'd never been late before. He'd always just been there. The rain was still falling. The canvas on my sandals was soaking and beginning to rub my heels so I stopped to take my shoes off. I wondered whether I could find Bracken's garage on my own. I should have paid more attention.

It wasn't because of work. I knew why he wasn't there.

Friday. I just had to find him and explain. I rehearsed the story as I walked. He'd laugh when I told him that Mrs OD had taken me captive on Dad's orders. He'd think it was funny that I'd had to play along to avoid detection.

It took forever to get to the station. I'd never walked the whole way before. I stopped at the phone box outside the entrance. If only I knew Bracken's number I could call him, but we'd never swopped numbers. I couldn't give him mine in case Dad answered and I'd never needed his because he was always just there, waiting for me.

I stepped into the booth, and it was a relief to be out of the rain. A puddle had begun to gather on the floor, but I plonked my bags down anyway and started flicking through the phone book. First I checked the ads in the yellow pages. 'G' for Garages and then 'M' for Mechanics and then finally, in desperation, 'E' for Engines and 'C' for Cars – but there was no listing for S. Bracken Autos. In the end, I found his home number in the white pages under 'B': S. Bracken, 4 The Glades. I didn't have any money so I'd have to reverse the charges – just as Dad had taught me to in case I was ever in trouble. This, I thought, counted as an emergency. The operator asked me for my name and then told me to stay on the line as she dialled his number. I could hear it ringing. Even though he was never home from the garage much before six with each ring, I expected him to answer. I needed him to answer. If not him, then Stella.

'There's no response, caller,' said the operator.

'Can you just try a bit longer?' I asked.

I could picture the phone ringing on the low table in the hall. I willed Bracken to answer. But then Bracken's words came back to me. 'It's only ever someone wanting money.' They never answered the phone.

I was exhausted. I let go of the phone. It dangled beside me.

'Caller, caller,' I could hear the operator saying.

My feet were sore. I sat on my bag to try to think things through. But I couldn't stop thinking horrible thoughts like:

Maybe he was dead.

Maybe his van had crashed on a slippery surface and his mum didn't know how to reach me.

Maybe he thought I didn't want him any more, or that I had to end it, and that's why I'd ignored him.

Maybe he'd left us, me and the baby, and was with someone prettier and sexier and more grown-up and less complicated.

Or maybe there had just been a horrible misunderstanding. The kind of misunderstanding that would destroy the rest of our lives – like in *Tess of the D'Urbervilles* when her letter got stuck under the carpet, and destroyed her and Angel's chance of living happily ever after. One moment of me failing to do the right thing and our future together had been extinguished.

It all felt hopeless. I started to shiver from the cold. I thought of the baby inside me and hoped it wasn't cold too. I thought of it tiny and alone in a huge dark space, unable to see or hear or say anything, and I began to cry. I cried for the baby, I cried for myself, I cried for how hopeless I felt and how messy it all was. Everything was so perfect a few days ago. I rested my head on my knees. Somewhere inside me I could hear my own sobbing but I couldn't make it stop.

Suddenly there was a rapping on the glass of the phone box and a blast of rain as the door opened.

'Excuse me,' said a woman's voice, 'are you using this phone or not?' and then, 'Rebecca? Rebecca Sedley, is that you? Whatever is the matter?'

I looked up to see Mary-Jane's mother standing above me. She seemed tall and far away. Her face was pretty like it always was, perfectly made-up, smooth and round and kind. She bent down and put her arms around me. I felt her warmth and breathed in the scent she always wore that made me think of flowers and Mum and everything soft and gentle and nice. I let myself collapse into her. I put my arms round her neck and although I was way too big I wished she'd pick me up and carry me so that I didn't have to feel the weight of everything else any longer.

'Whatever is the matter, my darling?' she asked. 'Come on, let's get you in the car.' She pulled me up and I wiped my eyes and straightened my skirt.

Her Mini was parked outside the phone box. 'I was just stopping to call home to make sure Mary-Jane was all right,' she explained. 'I try not to leave her alone these days, not even to do the shopping, but sometimes I have to.'

I tried to smile and think of what I could say that might make sense but nothing came to me so I just climbed into her car.

'Let's get the heating on,' she said. 'Your feet! Goodness gracious. Whatever were you thinking? We'll have you warm in no time. Lucky I stopped. Did you miss the bus or something?'

I nodded.

'You silly,' she said. 'It's not worth crying about.'

Warm air started blowing onto my feet and outside it was no longer raining.

'Was there no one at home? No one to come and get you?'

'I tried to reverse the charges but no one answered.'

'Poor love. Next time call me or better still just ask the school. They'll always find someone who can come and get you.'

I nodded again.

'You're just like Mary-Jane,' she said. 'Never wanting to ask for help in case it puts someone out.'

She chattered away as we drove out of town. She started with the weather and how no one was expecting the downpour, and then the second she'd got all the pleasantries done with she moved on to Mary-Jane and how ill she'd been. How she barely ate anything and was so weak that she spent her whole time sitting on her bed staring into space as if she was in a trance. Sometimes she didn't talk for days and days. I let her words wash over me hoping she didn't need a response. Mary-Jane was an idiot for being so unhappy when she had a mother like Mrs Hamilton to take care of her. I watched the countryside flash past the window.

I longed to lie down, to rest my head on Bracken's shoulder, to have him stroke my hair and tell me it would all be all right. I was so tired. I didn't want to think about anything any more, like where he was or what Mrs OD was going to do about my having given her the slip.

'I won't tell your Dad you missed the bus,' Mrs Hamilton said as she pulled into our driveway. 'I wouldn't want him getting cross with you over something so silly. But just do one thing for me, will you, darling? Call Mary-Jane. Or, better still, just come round and see her. I'll bake a cake. Maybe you can get through to her.'

'I will,' I said.

'She needs you right now, Rebecca. She needs her best friend.'

Chapter 34

I lost every last scrap of freedom. Dad kept me at home for the rest of the week and arranged for Mrs OD to bring work for me each day. After that he only allowed me back to school on condition that I was monitored continually by teachers. He said if I didn't comply it wouldn't be boarding school he sent me to but borstal.

I believed him.

I told myself not to panic. Once I could talk to Bracken everything would be sorted out. I knew it with a deep and absolute certainty.

I just had to bide my time and convince everyone I was a reformed character who appreciated the error of her ways. Then, the second they relaxed their grip, I'd get the chance to find Bracken. Or, maybe he'd come and find me. Maybe I would come out of school one day and there he'd be, leaning against his van wearing his shades and grinning his lopsided grin as if nothing had happened.

I did everything Dad and Mrs OD and school told me to.

At break and lunchtime I sat with Phelps's secretary or in the annexe of the staff room reserved for truants. In lessons I sat on my own in front of the teacher.

After school I helped Mrs OD tidy her precious lab and then climbed obediently into her car. I answered her questions about my revision and told her exactly what homework I had to do and did it. I even asked her how her day was, which made her stutter as she didn't know how to do small talk.

Every time I saw a white van or a tall dark-haired guy or anyone wearing a denim jacket on the way to or from school my heart leapt, like someone thirsty in the desert seeing an oasis in the distance. Only it was never him. It was always a mirage.

I didn't lose hope. Not for a second. I knew he'd come for me or I'd find him – it was just a question of time. Things that are real can't just disappear in an instant. It was basic science. Matter couldn't be destroyed and cease to exist.

I spent the evenings in my room while downstairs Dad played his opera recordings and drank. On my bedroom wall I pinned a detailed revision timetable. Revision became my refuge. A place I could hide while I waited for Bracken. I made a second chart on which I marked the days since I'd last seen him. I considered it a countdown until the day I'd see him again.

Hope kept me going.

I thought of the sailor's wife on the seashore scouring the horizon; the fiancée waiting for news from the front. What I was doing was no different. When a sailor was lost at sea or a private went missing in action, it was up to the woman who waited to keep him alive with her belief, so I kept Bracken alive with mine.

There was no loneliness because I knew that inside me, every day cells were multiplying and our baby was growing. I was desperate for the bump to finally show, so that I'd have visible proof that a part of Bracken existed.

At night, when I missed Bracken I talked to our baby. Our son, because I was even more certain it was going to be a boy. I told him that I loved him and that I would never let anything bad happen.

Sometimes I would think of Mary-Jane. I would think about asking Dad to let me call or visit her. I would wonder whether she was still sitting on her bed and whether her mum had persuaded her to eat. I would think about sitting with her and reading to her or putting on 10cc and trying to get her to dance. But then I'd think about the last time I'd visited. How she didn't want to hear anything about Bracken or what was happening in my life and I'd feel cross, let-down, abandoned. She wasn't the only one with problems. Friendship was a two-way thing.

Chapter 35

Eventually, just before term ended, my plan bore fruit. I was allowed to prove I could be trusted. I was allowed to catch the bus.

On the first morning, Pete was at the bus stop before me leaning against the pillar box blowing cigarette rings, his mouth opening and closing like a goldfish. He didn't say a word. It was just like old times. I ignored him back to show I didn't care.

I sat on the verge to wait but as soon as I'd taken my sandals off the bus came, which was odd because it was only 8.10. It was early. Les was never early, he was never even on time. He was always, without fail, reliably and perfectly late.

Pete got on first. So much for manners. I climbed on behind. The seat across the aisle from Les at the front was empty and I hesitated for a second, thinking maybe I'd sit there. Maybe it would be simpler than sitting with all the girls and trying to make Sal be nice to me so that everyone else wouldn't be catty.

I looked across to catch his eye and it was only then that I realized it wasn't Les at all. It was some weird old guy with a shaved head and a blue blazer and striped tie. I didn't like him. I could tell instantly, the way you can sometimes, that he wasn't a nice person.

'Oy, Becs.' Pen waved at me. 'You're back.'

'Who's that?' I slipped onto the seat next to Pen like I'd never been away.

'A right creep,' Marion said as she leant across the aisle.

'You're telling me.'

Sarah Slater came forward to join us and once Sal had got on we all huddled together like old times.

'Do you know where Les is?' I asked Sal.

Sal flicked her head towards the new guy. 'He won't say. Keeps saying he's our driver now so it doesn't matter what's happened to Les.'

'Reckon he's queer. Hasn't even bothered to learn any of our names,' said Sarah, who was letting her blonde dye grow out.

'I can tell you who's to blame,' I said. 'Fenella Jones. Her mum must have got him the sack.'

'It's just as much Dom's fault,' said Sarah and we all fell silent.

'You'd better say what you mean by that.' Sal stood up.

'I mean,' said Sarah calmly, 'that if Dom hadn't put that picture in Fenella Jones's bag Les might still be here. And if you, Sal, hadn't blabbed to him about Les being on the ID parade no one would have ever thought anything bad of him.'

There was a moment when nothing happened, like at the start of an album when the record is turning but no music comes out, and then before we knew it Sal was pulling Sarah's hair and punching at her head.

'Don't you fucking lay into my fella!' she screamed.

Sarah tried to duck out of the way but Sal grabbed her ponytail and pulled her head up so she couldn't protect herself. I knew I ought to get involved but I couldn't, not with the baby inside me. In the end it was Dom himself who broke it up.

'Ladies, ladies, what is going on here?' He pulled Sal off.

Sal spat and cursed but couldn't reach Sarah.

'Oy, you lot, sit down and be quiet,' a voice boomed from the front.

'Knob off,' shouted Dom.

Sal strained at Dom as he dragged her to the back of the bus with him. Sarah squished in next to me and buried her head in my lap.

'We didn't even say goodbye to Les,' she sobbed.

'He's not effing dead,' said Dave from the row behind.

'We know that,' Marion hissed at him.

'For all we know he could have got another job. We don't actually know what's happened,' Pen said sensibly.

'He wouldn't want another job,' I said. 'He needed the bus to take his son into town in his wheelchair.'

'I never thought I'd miss his Elvis tunes blaring out, but I do,' Pen said sadly.

'I miss his humbugs.' Marion smacked her rubbery lips together.

'Who am I going to flirt with now if Pete chucks me?' Sarah smiled.

It was a relief to be distracted for a moment, to be back

with the girls. But nothing was as it used to be. I rested a hand on my tummy. It wouldn't be long, I just had to get through that day's lessons and then I'd be able to find Bracken.

Chapter 36

I took the track through the park to the station. The main road wasn't safe. Anyone could've seen me and got their mum to offer me a lift or ask why I wasn't on the bus.

Once I'd passed the station I was safe. Nobody lived up this way. The pavement narrowed as the road rose to clear the railway line. Below a train cut through a tangle of tracks and wires. It was the sort of bridge that made you feel small and insignificant, like it wouldn't matter to anyone if you jumped.

The pavement ended at the industrial estate. This was not a place people came to on foot. The roads were full of identical buildings and were called names that accentuated everything they weren't, like 'Forest Road' and 'Violet Avenue'. Here and there cars were parked; on a newly tarmacked forecourt sat a small fleet of identical vans, on another a solitary digger but mostly it was empty.

When I got to the cul-de-sac my confidence started to wane. So far I'd only thought about the moment we were reunited, when he took me in his arms and kissed me and then buried his head in my hair and whispered that he loved me and that I was his sun and his moon and that he had barely lived without me. The happy ending.

But what happened if he'd changed his mind about me and the baby? What happened if he'd already found someone better? I twisted the ring round on my finger to prove to myself that it was real. I slowed down and tried to look composed. I didn't want him to see me hurrying like some silly, desperate schoolgirl.

As I rounded the bend the first thing I noticed was that the sign had gone and there was a high fence all the way along where the entrance should be. It was made from the sort of metal that was too thick to cut through, like they used around prisons and playgrounds.

Weirder still was that where the garage should have been there was just an empty space. Nothing. Way over at the back of the lot there was a small mound of rubble but that was it. A lone marker for something that no longer remained.

I pressed my forehead against the fence; the metal was still warm from the day's sun. In the distance a train sounded its horn as it rushed through to somewhere more important. I could make out the rectangle of concrete that used to be the forecourt but there were no cars, no tools, no building, no Bracken.

I followed the fence along until I found a gate set into it. High above it a sign read 'Henderson and Sons Estate Agents – FOR SALE OR TO LET'. Only someone had painted an 'I' between the 'O' and the 'T' so it said 'TOILET'.

I rattled the gate. It was padlocked and wouldn't budge so I slipped my sandals off and started climbing. I could only fit the very tips of my feet into the holes. I climbed next to one of the posts that held the mesh in place but the fence still started to wobble as I got higher. At the top I paused to catch my breath, swaying above the world. I remembered the trapeze artist in the sparkling pink leotard we'd seen walk the tightrope at Billy Smart's Circus once. My right foot slipped. I grabbed the post with both hands.

The fence was now swinging under my weight. Going back wasn't an option so I had to pick my way carefully down the inside of the fence, jumping the last few feet onto the ground.

It was imperative I stayed rational and logical. When Dad was working on a big case he always started with the facts – that's how all great mysteries were actually solved, he said. I started to search for clues. It looked like the concrete had been swept and someone had got rid of the weeds. There was a slight dip in the ground where the garage had stood, but aside from that and the mound of broken bricks there was nothing to prove the garage or Bracken had ever existed.

'Hey, carrot hair.'

I jumped guiltily. A man with a T-shirt that was way too short for his beer belly was standing by the fence.

'What do you think you're doing? That's private property.'

'Sorry,' I shouted back. 'I was just looking.'

'Get out now or I'll be calling the police.'

I went to climb back over the fence but he unlocked the gate. 'I'm sorry,' I said. 'What happened to the garage?'

'Garage, is that what you call it?' he snorted, pulling a large dirty hanky out of his pocket and wiping his forehead with it. 'Plot's worth a lot more without it than with, I'll tell you that much. Anyhow what's a nice-sounding girl like you doing breaking and entering?'

'I'm sorry,' I repeated.

'I think you'd better come with me so we can discuss the matter with your parents.'

'Got to go,' I said backing away and then I turned and legged it back up the dead end.

Chapter 37

I'd never hitchhiked before. After school the next day I walked to the start of the road that led to Stansted and then stuck my thumb out. I thought the first car that saw me would stop. But it didn't and neither did any of the others that hurtled past after it. A couple of drivers honked and flashed their lights; a green Morris Marina slowed down and a bloke wolf-whistled out the window, but no one stopped. I was about to give up and walk the whole way when a huge lorry pulled over.

'Where you going, love?' the driver said. He was young with spiky ginger hair and a giant spider's web tattoo that covered one of his stringy arms.

'The Glades, it's much further along. I can tell you where.' I was so relieved someone had stopped that I didn't allow myself to think about whether he was safe or not. I just hopped in.

'Call me Dave,' he said, like his name could be something else. Then he offered me some Wrigleys and started telling me how his lorry was five tons and articulated with its own sleeping quarters in the cab behind the seats. I tried to remember the details to tell Bracken later.

Eventually I spotted the smart house with the pillars and I asked Dave to pull over just after it.

Once the lorry had disappeared I walked up the last stretch to Bracken's house. His white van was outside. I was in luck, he was home already. I couldn't help myself when I saw it, I just started running up the hill. I didn't care if I looked desperate.

As I approached the door the dogs started barking. I'd never been so happy to hear them.

'Hey you sillies, it's only me. No need to make a fuss,' I shouted, knocking eagerly on the door.

The lounge curtains were closed. I knocked again. I hoped they weren't pretending to be out.

I knocked a third time. The dogs were going nuts. After what felt like an eternity I heard Stella inside shooing them away.

'Who is it?' she.yelled.

'It's me. Me, Becs.'

The dogs started barking again and I heard her scream, 'Get in the sodding kitchen.' And then, finally, she opened the door.

Stella's hair looked like it hadn't been washed for days. She stood in the doorway. I went to hug her but then I stopped myself. She wasn't smiling.

'You've got a cheek turning up here. Who do you think you are?'

'Is Bracken here?' I mumbled.

'Jesus Christ,' she said and closed the door.

I tucked my shirt in and loosened my shirt button so a neat triangle of flesh was showing. I pulled a couple of wisps of hair from my ponytail to hang on either side of my face.

The door opened again, but it wasn't Bracken, it was Stella with a lit fag in her hand. One of the greyhounds poked its head through her legs. I bent down to stroke him but Stella kicked him back inside.

'So Miss La-di-da wants to see Stephen, does she? Wants her bit of rough? Well, she'll have to wait a good few years.' Behind her, I could see the heap of shoes in the hallway.

'What do you mean? His van's here.' I pointed at it as if that would help. 'I went to the garage but it's not there any more. Someone's pulled it down. We had a misunderstanding. Has something happened? Has there been an accident?' I started to cry.

She shook her head. 'You're on another planet. You've got no sodding clue. Think you can swan into people's lives and take what you want, it's all a game like one of your story books.'

A plane hummed in the distance overhead. In one of the neighbouring houses a door banged and someone shouted. I didn't know what to say.

Stella's face suddenly softened. Just like Bracken's did after he'd lost his temper. 'Just go home where you belong, Becs. You've caused enough trouble. You're not welcome here any more.'

Before I could work out what to say she'd shut the door. I raised my hand to knock again but I didn't dare so I just stood there staring at the closed door, trying to make sense of what she'd said.

Eventually I walked down the path to the road, to Bracken's van. It was locked. I peeked through the window. Everything looked normal inside. I could even see a Wagon Wheel wrapper that I must have forgotten to throw away in the footwell of the passenger seat. I walked round to the back of the van and tried the handle. That was locked too.

The white of the van was grey with dust. I tore a page out of my French vocab book and wrote: 'Please please come and get me. I need you. Don't worry about Dad. I'll be waiting.' I added my address at the bottom in case Bracken had forgotten where I lived and folded it up and secured it under the windscreen wiper.

Stella appeared at the door again.

'Clear off,' she shouted. 'I told you. Clear off and don't come back.'

Chapter 38

Term ended and I didn't see anyone, I didn't call anyone, I didn't go out. I stayed locked in my room listening to 'Space Oddity', trying to revise and waiting for Bracken to come and find me.

No one called. I didn't get invited to anything. Maybe they were all working or they'd just forgotten about me.

The only person who did ring was Mary-Jane's mum. She spoke to Dad.

'Don't you want to visit her?' he asked. 'Mrs Hamilton seems to think Mary-Jane would benefit from seeing you.'

'I'm working. I thought that's what you wanted me to do,' I snapped.

When the isolation got too much I'd creep into the garden and lie on the grass under the shade of the apple tree that was meant to have been the start of Mum's orchard. There was some broken rope hanging from one of the branches where there used to be a swing.

The garden shed was just to my right. It was a bit more

than a shed really. According to Dad it was actually a folly, a mini version of our house, complete with latticed windows, red bricks and a neat gabled roof. It was almost big enough to be someone's home. Inside it smelt of damp peat and stored apples. Nat, Dad's gardener, had made shelves on which everything was neatly marked and stored. Garden tools, seeds, plant ties, nuts, bolts. You name it, there was a place for it.

From beyond the shed I heard an engine throb into life. Moments later Nat drove by on a small red tractor, dragging the mower up the lawn, leaving ordered stripes of shorn grass in his wake. He was young. Younger than Bracken by a good few years. I'd never really thought about him before. I didn't know anything about his life; he was just the guy who did what Dad should be doing. If anyone at school knew we had a gardener it would be the end. When Nat had finished mowing he emptied the lawn clippings from the trailer into a big pile ready for burning. The smell was comforting.

'All right for some,' he called over. 'Haven't you got anything better to do?'

I picked up the Biology textbook I'd brought out with me and pretended to read.

'What about your friends? Good-looking girl like you should be out having fun.'

'I've got exams, I'm revising.'

'All work and no play,' he grinned.

I got up and walked back to my room.

It was Mrs Turner who noticed. It was a Friday afternoon and I'd come down from my room to make a sandwich for lunch.

I'd got the loaf of bread on a board on the kitchen table and some lettuce and tomato and cheese all laid out along with a large glass of milk. I'd been drinking as much milk as possible so the baby's bones would be strong. I'd told Dad I needed it so my brain would work for the exams and he'd been ordering an extra bottle of full fat from the milkman for me every day. Mrs Turner was standing at the sink with her back to me.

'Not come on then?' she asked.

'Pardon?' I tried not to tear the bread as I spread the cold butter.

'Your periods.'

I knocked the glass of milk over.

'Have you got a cloth?' I asked her.

'I'll get that. Now you, sit down and tell me what's been going on.'

'I don't know what you mean.'

'I'm not stupid.' She wrung a cloth out and started to wipe up the milk. 'You haven't had a period for at least two months. All your sanitary towels are in the bathroom cupboard untouched. You're drinking milk like it's going out of fashion. You haven't been out with your friends for weeks.'

I felt myself blushing as I stared at the table.

'Is it Pete?' she asked. 'Don't worry, you wouldn't be the first one, if it is.'

I pretended I couldn't hear her.

'Why do you think he got booted out of his fancy school?'

I went back to spreading butter on the bread.

'You don't have to tell me. But you're going to have to do something sooner or later before your dad finds out. He'll turn you into minced meat. Pure and simple.'

She came over to my side of the table and put an arm round me. 'Look, love, you're not the first girl to get yourself into trouble. But you can't just ignore it.'

'I'm not,' I mumbled.

'Not what? Ignoring it or in trouble?'

'Neither.'

Mrs Turner took her arm off my shoulders and went back to the sink. 'Fine, have it your way.' She turned the tap on and then off again. 'Don't lie to me, Rebecca. Or it won't just be your Dad you're reckoning with.'

From then on I made sure I avoided Mrs Turner. I pinned a notice on my bedroom door saying 'No entry. Do not disturb', and if she was in the house I simply didn't come out.

About a week later an envelope appeared under my bedroom door. It said 'Private' in Mrs Turner's familiar half capitals. Inside there was a leaflet wrapped in a note, which said, 'This is where we took our Jean when she got into trouble. I can take you if you want.' It was from some clinic that specialized in unwanted pregnancies. A young woman smiled out from the cover.

I thought about how angry Bracken had got when I'd suggested an abortion. I rested a hand on my tummy. I couldn't imagine wanting to get rid of our baby. Especially not now that it was the only bit of Bracken I had left. I took the leaflet and shoved it in the bin.

Chapter 39

The day the call came I'd woken up early thinking about Bracken. The sky was a clear blue, it was going to be another scorcher. Dad shouted for me to come down for breakfast but I closed my eyes again and imagined I was at the reservoir with Bracken. We'd climbed to the ledge halfway up the water tower and were sunbathing. I'd just finished reading to him and he was gently shielding my face from the sun so I didn't get too burnt and telling me that I shouldn't hate my freckles because they were like stars, each one a bright and precious universe.

'Breakfast,' Dad shouted again. He should have been on his way to work, not harassing me.

And then the phone rang, which was odd. It was early. Before eight. Nobody ever called at that hour.

For some reason I thought it might be Bracken and so I raced down to try to get to it before Dad. But by the time I'd got to the kitchen he'd already answered it. He waved at me to leave the room, swatting at me urgently as if I was an unwelcome fly, and when I hesitated he covered the receiver with his hand, and barked, 'Out. Now.'

I hovered outside the door. I couldn't make out who he was talking to but I did hear him say 'Oh dear' and 'I'm so terribly sorry', and then he asked what he could do to help and whether there was a date yet.

He wouldn't tell me what'd happened. He said we'd talk when he got back from court, the same as he used to say when I was little and in trouble and wanted to know what my punishment was. I returned to my room and tried to revise. There was a sensation in my stomach, like something very delicate was falling and I couldn't move quickly enough to catch it. I sat at my desk but couldn't concentrate.

From the garden I could hear the electric whine and release of a chain saw. When the sound finally stopped, wisps of smoke spiralled up from the bottom of the garden. Outside I found Nat heaping armfuls of yesterday's grass cuttings onto a small bonfire. The fire sparked and spat as the damp cuttings hit the flames.

'Had to take a branch off.' He pointed over to the solitary apple tree.

A newly sawn stump had taken the place of the branch that used to hold the rope for the swing.

'You shouldn't have. That was Mum's tree.'

'Sorry,' Nat shrugged, and then continued heaping clippings onto the fire. 'Nature's nature, though,' he said after a time. He was wearing a grey Levi's T-shirt and his skin was tanned.

'Meaning?'

'That if something's dead, there's nothing you can do about it.'

When I didn't reply he wandered back to the shed. I sat cross-legged and watched the flames until finally the embers died down.

As I headed back to the house Nat called to me from the front of the shed where he was sitting reading the paper.

'Fancy a cuppa? I've made a pot.'

I couldn't face returning to my books so I nodded and wandered over.

He folded the paper and gestured to me to sit on his chair, the pink-and-white folding one that Mum had bought for picnics.

'Won't take a jiffy,' he said. 'Sugar?'

'Two, please.'

He went into the shed and I picked up the paper. On the front page was a grainy black-and-white photo of the pond where I'd camped with Mary-Jane and her dad.

'Tea's up.' Nat held out an orange mug.

It was too hot to drink so I rested it on the grass and turned back to the paper. 'MILL POND TRAGEDY' read the headline and then beneath that: '*Local teen found by parents just before dawn.*'

Nat took the paper from me and folded it open to the next page, saying, 'Isn't that uniform from your school?'

Chapter 40

It wasn't Mary-Jane. I told myself that the grainy picture on the second page was just an arrangement of black-and-white dots in the shape of a face with a school tie and a white shirt bolted onto the bottom for good measure.

The photo was of a stranger.

I closed my eyes to see the real Mary-Jane, but when I did I could only picture her in pieces. Her green eyes. Her long thin legs. The corner of her smile. Her head resting on her knees. The swish of her hair when she danced. I tried not to close my eyes after that.

Mrs Turner said I should go into school. That's where everyone was, hugging and holding and crying. But I couldn't.

When the funeral came Dad wouldn't let me go. He said it wasn't appropriate. It would be too upsetting coming so close to my exams. But he went and, according to Mrs Turner who went too, he helped to carry the coffin and read a lesson from the Bible about love.

I picked some forget-me-nots and made a small posy but when I got near to Mary-Jane's house I was crying so hard I had to turn back.

Chapter 41

The bleeding started the following week.

When she saw the sheets, Mrs Turner called the doctor out and made me lie down until he came.

Dr Tunnell coughed as he entered my room. His were the first human hands to touch me when I slithered into this world onto my parents' master bed so he had literally known me all my life. On account of that fact together with his long beak-like nose Mum had christened him 'The Stork', which was ironic in the current circumstances.

He ushered Mrs Turner out of the room and then muttered for a bit about how much he cared for both my parents irrespective of who had done what. He tugged on his cuffs and put on his pince-nez and finally asked me whether I'd had sex. Only, he didn't use the word sex – he said 'intercourse' instead.

I stared at the ceiling. 'My best friend drowned herself.'

'Anything you tell me won't leave the confines of this room. In other words I'm happy to keep this conversation confidential. I won't tell your father anything you don't want me to.'

I closed my eyes.

'Rebecca, I need to know what's happened. It would be most unusual to lose this amount of blood spontaneously. As you know, there have been a number of unfortunate occurrences recently. If something has happened I need you to tell me.'

'No, nothing like that. I promise.'

Dr Tunnell looked relieved and said 'good' in a matter-of-fact way as if we'd just decided that the weather was particularly clement for this time of year. He told me I needed to rest and then folded his glasses and inserted them back into the breast pocket of his navy jacket out of which was poking a neatly folded polka-dot hankie.

He hovered awkwardly for a moment by the door. 'You know you can always talk to me, don't you, Rebecca? Should the need ever arise.'

I nodded.

I heard his footsteps on the stairs and then the front door bang shut behind him.

I wanted to call after him to please come back. I wanted to ask him whether the bleeding meant the baby definitely had gone or whether there was anything he could do to save his life. But I didn't call after him. I didn't need to because I knew.

Dad kept trying to persuade me to visit Mary-Jane's mum but I couldn't.

I stayed in bed. I refused to allow the curtains to be opened. I said I felt too unwell. Every so often he popped into my room with a glass of milk or a sandwich like he was worried I was going to go the same way as Mary-Jane. Like it was contagious.

At night when I closed my eyes I saw Mary-Jane floating face down in a polka-dot anorak that had air trapped under it so that it ballooned up so her back was afloat while her mouth and nose were under the surface breathing in water.

I dreamt of her and of the baby and sometimes it was her that was floating and sometimes it was the baby and sometimes Les's son Ian was in the water too strapped in and sinking in his wheelchair and sometimes Mary-Jane was not floating but walking towards me on top of the water like Jesus with her stick-thin arms and it was only when she'd got right up close that I realized she was a skeleton and her limbs were just bones because all her flesh had rotted or been eaten and then I'd wake up screaming.

Some nights I was in court. I stood in the dock while a deep booming voice that sounded like Dad listed the charges against me. Crimes like:

Not saving Mary-Jane from drowning.

Not visiting her.

Not calling her.

Using her as an alibi so I could see Bracken when she was sitting mute and alone on her bed.

Not keeping secrets. Telling everyone about the identity parade when I'd promised not to.

Not staying the night at her house any more when she asked me to.

Not listening to 10cc unless I had to.

Acting like she was uncool and immature.

Letting Sal be my best friend.

Not telling her that I loved her.

Not spending every second that I could with her while she was still alive.

Then the voice boomed out the secondary charges. The less obvious offences. The cowardly, lazy ones. The crimes of omission like:

Letting Fenella Jones get bullied off the bus.

Not standing up for Les.

Not being kind to Dad.

Then, often, my dream would shift from the courtroom back to the Mill Pond and I'd see Ian sinking in his wheel-chair, which would have got tangled up with Mary-Jane who was always lying face down in the water.

When I woke up I couldn't shake the thought that I was the common factor in all that had gone wrong. I had failed to act. And then I'd think of Mum and wonder whether if I'd been a different child she might have stayed with Dad.

Chapter 42

Two weeks before I was meant to be sitting my O levels Pen came to see me. Dad showed her up to my room and she was already through the door before I could point out that I didn't allow any visitors.

'What's going on?' she asked, flopping onto my beanbag. 'Can't have you losing the will to go on too.'

I shrugged.

'You know they've caught him, don't you?'

'Who?'

'The perv. They caught him. Day of Mary-Jane's funeral. Mum says it was a tragic irony.'

I made a face.

'Some sex maniac who'd only been out of jail a few months. Caught him in the school car park apparently, offering a girl a lift. The grey hair was a wig. Wasn't real. That's why they didn't get him earlier, kept thinking they were looking for an old bloke. Taken him to London for trial as they say he won't get a fair one here.'

'Does that mean they gave Les his job back?'

Pen shook her head. 'Sal saw him signing on. Had his son with him. I never knew he was crippled.'

I started to cry but Pen didn't notice because she was pacing the room in mid-flow.

'They should be doing that bloke for murder. If he hadn't done what he did to Mary-Jane she'd still be here.'

Pen stopped in front of my bookshelf and tapped the revision timetable that was pinned to the wall beside it. 'Jesus, Becs. Learnt it all yet?'

She read out the list of topics on my timetable in a silly voice that sounded a bit like Mr Phelps when he was listing the names of people with detentions in Assembly, which made me laugh. And I realized how long it had been since I'd seen anyone apart from Dad and Mrs Turner and the inside of my own mind.

Next she spotted my other chart, the one where I'd crossed off the days since I'd last seen Bracken.

'What's this one?'

And before I knew it I was telling her. I was telling her everything, the whole story, and she was listening and nodding and tutting and it felt so good to speak; so good not to be alone with it all. And when I'd finished I sat looking at her with her sensible brown hair and pale-blue eyes and waited. I waited for her verdict, to see if she could piece together what had happened, why Bracken had left me and when he might come back.

Pen paused and looked at me. 'Do you really want to know what I think?'

I nodded.

'He's gone, Becs. It's that simple. Mum always says trust is the most important thing.'

'But I do trust him,' I protested. 'We're engaged.'

'But he's gone. He's scarpered. He left you pregnant without a word. You're a loony. How can you trust someone like that?'

'There's got to be a reason. It's what I believe.'

'Think yourself lucky. Thank God you're not still pregnant. Can you imagine? Can you imagine telling your dad?'

She walked over to my window and opened the curtains. The sunlight blazed in.

'It's already the hottest summer on record and you're lying in a dark room moping about some bloke who's never coming back.' She walked over and sat beside me on the bed. 'Everything does happen for a reason,' she said, 'but just not always the reason that you want it to be.'

Chapter 43

When the exams were over Pen dragged me to The Three Crowns across from school. She said she needed to have a 'proper talk' and picked a table in the corner of the Lounge Bar.

I doodled on the beer mat while Pen bought us each a lemonade shandy. The barman had a large barrel belly and winked at me every time I looked up. Bracken would've said shandy was gnat's piss but Pen wouldn't risk ordering anything stronger. She nearly didn't get me one as I still wasn't legal being only fifteen, eleven months and thirteen days, but I said I wouldn't let her have her 'proper talk' unless she did.

'I'm worried you'll freak out and get angry with me.' She put the drinks down carefully in front of us.

'Do you remember how Fenella Jones's mum thought the perv was Les?'

'Of course,' I said. 'And we never did anything to stop them sacking him like we should've.' I brought my glass down hard on the table for emphasis. 'We should have stood up for him, protested, done something. We just let her ruin his life.'

'That's not what I meant.' Pen looked uneasy and still hadn't had a sip of her drink. 'Look, I don't want you to think I'm like Fenella Jones's mum, that's all, you know, pointing the finger.'

'Pen, how on earth could I think that? Look at yourself for starters.'

We both laughed. Pen couldn't look less like a hippy with her tidy straight hair and sensible shoes. Her mum wouldn't even let her wear jeans. And she was the only girl in our year, apart from me, who hadn't been allowed to have her ears pierced.

'It's about Bracken. We've all been thinking. I mean, have you ever thought about what a coincidence it is that he disappeared and then they found the sicko? I mean, I know it's a long shot but—'

'What are you saying?' I stood up.

'Calm down – please, Becs. This is why I was scared of saying it.'

'Go on, say it. Get it over with.'

'All right, I will. Did you ever think maybe, you know, maybe Bracken was the guy, I mean…'

I didn't stay to listen to the end of her sentence.

I walked straight out of the pub and I didn't stop when she called after me.

It took nearly two hours to get to Bracken's house, so it was late, maybe nearly midnight by the time I arrived. The moon was full, just like it had been the night Bracken had first brought me there, and the small row of houses was bathed in a pale half-light.

Looking up at the house I could see the curtains in Bracken's room were open, making his window look like a simple geometric shape. A black rectangular hole. He never would have touched those girls, not in a million years.

His van was still there with one tyre so flat that its hub was resting on the road. A bunch of flyers and leaflets offering special deals on things no one ever wanted had accumulated under the windscreen wipers. I found my note resting untouched beneath them.

I started walking up towards the front door but, before I got there, the barking started. The dogs strained and bashed against the door. Set against the stillness of the night they sounded savage, malign. I was scared.

I banged on the door. 'It's me, Becs,' I shouted.

The dogs kept barking. Nobody came. The moon went behind a cloud so the only light was from the street-lamp behind me.

I banged again. And when still nobody came I banged and banged and shouted till my fist was sore and my throat hurt.

Next door an upstairs window opened. 'What the fuck are you doing?' a voice shouted. 'Shut your effing face or I'll do it for you.'

I turned around and walked quickly back up the path. When I got to the main road I started to run. I ran beyond the glow of the streetlight into where the darkness began; through the looming shadows cast by trees and telegraph poles; past the drive to the house with the white pillars.

I ran with my lungs burning for air, until long after my legs had told me to stop. I ran through walls of pain until I was beyond anything that could hurt me.

When I did eventually stop I realized something had shifted. My head was no longer full of chatter. The night air felt still and cold. I was calm. I was clear. It was simple: I couldn't do it any more.

I couldn't keep believing in someone who wasn't there.

I'd believed in Mum.

I'd believed in Bracken.

They'd both left me.

Mary-Jane had gone too.

Enough was enough.

If someone really loved you, they didn't leave.

Chapter 44

St Anthony's held an open evening just before the end of term. I took Pen's arm as we walked through the large stone arch into the courtyard of the sixth form college. We were the only two of our lot there because we were the only two doing A levels. At the far end, through another arch we could see playing fields and tennis courts stretching into the distance.

A boy with a rash of red acne and a Prefect badge showed us round the common rooms where you were allowed to make tea and coffee and hang out during free periods and break. St Anthony's had been a boys' grammar and was only just going co-ed. Pen looked a little uncertain when the spotty boy told us there'd be four of him for every one of us. He left us outside the sports hall, which smelt of socks and chlorine and had huge glass walls that opened in the summer onto its own pool.

Inside, the teachers had set up trestle tables: one for each subject. Pen's parents wanted her to be a doctor so she headed

215

off to investigate the Biology stand, which was surrounded by lots more boys in need of Clearasil. I'd chosen English, History and Latin. 'Good for law,' Dad had said, to which I'd replied, 'Dream on.'

The English stall had rows of novels and poetry collections neatly laid out like a second-hand bookshop. I picked up something by Hardy and flicked through it so I wouldn't look like an idiot for not knowing anybody.

'Read anything by him?' I looked up and there was this guy with thick dark curly hair and deep-blue eyes standing in front of me, grinning.

'Only *Tess*,' I said, feeling myself blush. He looked really cute and was wearing faded jeans that reminded me of Bracken's. I liked the fact he hadn't got all dressed up for the evening to impress the teachers.

'And? What did you think?'

'Not a very happy ending,' I heard myself mumble.

'Can't mess with fate,' he replied and gave me another grin.

Then a bell rang and we were ushered to the Assembly hall, which felt more like a chapel than a school as it had stained glass. Streamers and balloons hung from the walls and a big banner read 'Welcome to St Anthony's'.

At the far end, on a small stage three shaggy-haired boys bashed away on electric guitars while a fourth sang moodily into a mic. They'd never have allowed anything like this at the comp. Pen and I stood and watched for a while and then wandered over to a table loaded up with Tizer and lemonade and Hula Hoops.

The guy serving drinks was dishy. His checked shirt had

the top three buttons undone and from the chain around his neck dangled a star just like the one David Essex wore. It was only when he looked up and asked us what we'd like that I realized it was the guy I'd spoken to about Hardy.

'You again,' he smiled.

'Fate.' I smiled back.

'Well, you're going to be seeing a lot more of me next year.'

'You doing English too?'

'Kind, of,' he laughed. 'I teach it.'

'You're kidding. Sorry, I thought you were a pupil.'

He held out his hand. 'Dave. Dave Cooper, your English teacher.'

'Nice to meet you.'

He gave me another grin and I saw he had dimples. Someone pushed in wanting a drink so Pen and I headed back into the middle of the hall. The band had finished and 'I Love to Boogie' was playing so we both started dancing.

'You're in there,' said Pen.

'He's a teacher.'

'So what? He liked you. Anyway, he's younger than Bracken was.'

That night as I lay in bed, I started to feel excited. Maybe life wouldn't be so bad after all. Maybe one day there would be other people in the world that I could fancy and maybe at some distant point on the horizon I would get over Bracken.

Chapter 45

I'm not sure how but somehow I managed to persuade Dad to let me go InterRailing with Pen and her big sister during the summer holidays. Dad agreeing to his only child traipsing around Europe was obviously a major miracle that alone should have seen our house converted into a shrine, but then another even more significant miracle happened.

Dad stopped drinking.

After Mary-Jane had died he'd banished whisky from the house. I hadn't taken it seriously. There'd been short periods when he'd tried to stop before but this time it held. He hadn't touched a drop. He instructed Nat to move the mahogany drinks cabinet that was in his study to the shed. Nat balanced it on his wheelbarrow, which left a trail of mud through the house, but for once Mrs Turner didn't complain.

Now that Dad wasn't drinking, he wanted to talk in the evenings and got all enthusiastic about my trip, which was simultaneously endearing and irritating. He bought a huge map of Europe from Smiths and hung it on the wall of his study right where the drinks cabinet had been. He told me to stick pins into the places I was intending to visit and then read to me in great detail about them from his *Encyclopaedia Britannica*.

Finally, I began to see what might have made Mum love him all those years ago. Underneath all his pontificating he wasn't so bad really.

Having said that, he forgot my birthday so he wasn't totally perfect but it didn't matter because turning sixteen was hardly the milestone I'd hoped it would be now that Bracken wasn't around any more.

On the day, I packed a picnic lunch and rode my bike out to the reservoir. On the way I stopped and bought myself a packet of salt-and-vinegar Chipsticks as a birthday treat. I felt guilty as I climbed the metal rungs up the water tower, like I was going back in time and deceiving Dad and Pen and everyone who wanted me to get on with my life and be a worldly success, but I needed to spend that day with Bracken or, if not with him, then at least with his memory.

The family of falcons had long gone but the nest remained. I sat on the ledge next to the bits of broken rubble and concrete. The sky was a flawless blue. Sitting high above the dried-out reservoir I tried to get a better perspective on my life.

There were some things I couldn't change, like:

Mum leaving and Mary-Jane dying.

There were some things I couldn't know, like:

Why Bracken had disappeared.

Why some random stranger picked our village to start assaulting girls.

Why Mary-Jane hadn't been able to get over what happened like the others had.

But there were other things I could do something about and I resolved there and then that I would.

I ate my cheese-and-tomato sandwich avoiding the crusts and then nibbled my Chipsticks slowly. Just as I'd managed to get twenty-six tiny bites out of my second to last one, the shadow of a bird passed overhead.

I scattered the crusts of my sandwich beside the abandoned nest and climbed back down to my bike as quickly and quietly as I could. Standing in the dry grass beside the road, I watched as the falcon swooped down to the nest for the bread. 'Those are from Bracken,' I shouted up to it.

The next day, I persuaded Dad to write a legal letter to the Council asking that Lesley Robbins be reappointed as a bus driver. Dad said it really wasn't any of our business but that it did sound like an open-and-shut case of unfair dismissal.

'He may not want his job back,' Dad pointed out as he reluctantly scrawled his signature across the bottom of the letter in thick black ink.

'But at least this way he'll have the choice,' I said.

Dad shook his head but stuck stamps on the envelope anyway and then put it in his briefcase to post.

Then I picked some yellow roses from the garden and put them into the basket of my bicycle.

Mary-Jane's lane was awash with summer colours. Foxgloves, poppies, cow parsley and hawthorn all jostled chest-high grass for space on the verges. I stopped to add some to the roses to make it a proper bouquet. The light shone through the canopy of green leaves above. Each inch of the journey was so familiar that it felt like forever and no time at all since I'd last been there.

I wondered whether Mrs Hamilton would shout at me when she saw me and ask Mr Hamilton to tell me to leave. If she didn't, if she did let me come in, I'd hug her and cry and tell her I was so sorry but after that I wasn't quite sure what I'd say.

It felt inconceivable as I pedalled up the last bit of hill that Mary-Jane wouldn't just be there too, sitting in her bedroom or drawing or practising some new dance routine that she'd just dreamt up. It didn't make sense that she could just stop existing.

It was only after I'd rested my bike against the wooden fence and my heart had started to pound and a feeling that I might be sick had started to rise up from my tummy that I noticed the car parked just outside. A red estate. The Hamiltons must have visitors, or maybe they were out because their Mini wasn't there, or maybe they'd got a new car.

At the far end of the garden a toddler in blue shorts and a stripy top was trying to ride a small trike. He shrieked as it tipped over.

A woman with short curly hair raced across the lawn from the back door.

'Is Mrs Hamilton in?' I called out to her.

'Moved out last week,' she shouted back over her shoulder as she picked up the boy.

I didn't allow myself to cry. Grief was like a trapdoor I couldn't afford to let myself fall through.

Chapter 46

Out of the blue, Dad announced he was holding a garden party. He invited all our neighbours, even Pete's parents, and allowed me to ask my friends.

Nat spent days beforehand getting the garden ready, trimming the hedges, re-mowing the already perfect lawns and weeding the flowerbeds. Ours was the only garden that wasn't parched and brown thanks to Dad's refusal to observe the hosepipe ban. He said no town-hall official was going to tell him what he could and couldn't do on his own land.

The day before the party, Mrs OD arrived in a floral dress, lipstick and a pair of court shoes. Dad led her into the study and shortly afterwards a removals lorry pulled into the drive.

'Mind the paintwork,' Dad barked as two men in white overalls carried the glass display cases containing his butterfly collection out of the house.

'Mrs O'Dwyer has kindly agreed to house the collection in her laboratory,' Dad explained as Mrs OD gave me an embarrassed smile.

Dad hired a bartender called Albert who wore a black jacket and bow tie and spoke with a French accent. Mrs Turner and her daughter Jean were on hand to serve the guests. They both had small frilly white aprons, and were instructed to circulate with silver platters of cocktail sausages and small cucumber sandwiches. Even Nat smartened up for the occasion. He wore a suit and handed out glasses of wine on a tray. Noticing how handsome he looked made me feel like I was being unfaithful to Bracken so I tried to ignore him.

Dad let me use his record player and gave me an extension lead so I could play music at the far end of the garden where it wouldn't bother the grown-ups. I decorated the glade with tea lights in glasses so that it looked really magical.

Just before the party started Dad took me aside and, after clearing his throat a few times, said, 'Rebecca, if she were here today, your mother would be very proud.'

The 'younger generation', as Dad referred to us, sat under the apple tree listening to music. Even Sal and Dom turned up arm in arm with a giant can of Watneys in a plastic bag.

We talked about what was going to happen next for each of us. What the future would hold. Sal had got a job as an apprentice in the hairdressers by the bandstand. The money was pretty rubbish but it'd be fine once she started getting tips. Dom was going to the Tech. A few others were signing on. Pete was off to some boarding school in Scotland for his final two years. Pen and I were off to St Anthony's and then, hopefully, university.

No one mentioned Mary-Jane, but she was there. Her death hovered in the gaps, as we casually chatted about what we wanted for our lives.

Mary-Jane didn't get to have a future. She'd didn't get to see how things turned out.

'Stop thinking,' said Pen who was sitting beside me. 'I can hear the cogs turning from here.'

'What?' said Marion.

'She's just thinking too much,' said Pen. 'Makes her unhappy.'

''Bout what?' asked Marion.

'What might have been,' I said.

'Oh for God's sake, give it a break,' said Dom.

And I did. No more thinking about 'what might have been'. I made myself concentrate on 'what was'. What actually existed. All of us sitting around laughing and chatting under the tree, and it wasn't so bad after all.

'Drinks anyone?' Nat crouched down beside us with a tray full of glasses of cold white wine.

'It's a hard life,' said Sal, taking one.

Nat gave me a wink as he went to refill the tray.

'I'm going to have my own personal butler one day,' announced Pete.

'Oh shut up,' said Dom, thumping him on his arm.

Then before I knew it we were all piling on top of Pete. Girls and boys. 'Bundle, bundle,' everyone was shouting and it was just like nothing bad had ever happened.

We stayed outside as the sky darkened and stars began to appear. Everyone was a bit drunk but no one was out of hand. Most of the grown-ups had already left. I lay back on the grass, closed my eyes, relaxed into the ground and let the world slowly spin. When I opened them again the sky was dark as ink and speckled with light from other solar systems.

Pretty Thing

The moon was a tiny crescent of new life. I couldn't remember feeling this peaceful for months. But then I pictured Bracken, somewhere else, looking up at the same night sky – and the moment was gone.

Chapter 47

The letter arrived on the morning I was due to leave for Europe. My bedroom was in a terrible state. There were clothes all over the floor. Pen's mum had told us we should only take what we could fit into a backpack and mine just wasn't big enough for all the stuff I wanted to take. So far I'd shoved in new shorts and gold sandals and way too many books. I was wearing my jeans and cheesecloth shirt but beyond that I didn't know how to choose what to take and what to leave behind.

It came in a small brown envelope, like the ones Dad used when he was paying bills, and it had my name in capitals on the front. Someone had scribbled out the address in a blue biro and written 'Try Number 12'. I looked through the scribble and saw that whoever had sent it thought I lived at Number 21. The postmark was from before my O levels.

Inside was a piece of lined paper filled with small messy writing I didn't recognize.

There was also an official-looking white card with 'Her Majesty's Prison Chelmsford' printed across the top and then lots of information about how to visit.

I read the letter first.

Red,

I've written so many letters and never sent them because I thought probably the best thing I could do was to let you get on with your life without me. But when Mum said you'd been round I knew you hadn't given up on me. That there was still hope for you and me and the baby and that maybe you could forgive me.

I sat down on the beanbag. For a second, maybe only a fraction of a horrible second, I thought that perhaps Pen and the others had been right. That it had been him. But it was only for a split second.

I read on. It was Coventry. He'd been an idiot, he wrote, he should have known the money was too good to be true.

I'm so sorry. I did the job to make things better for you. I'd never have got involved if I'd known it was bent gear. Mum says you can live with her till I'm out and then I'll make it up to you. I promise. For the rest of your life.

He put a PS at the bottom asking me to send a photo and to visit as soon as I could.

I folded the piece of paper in half and slipped it inside my bra. Then I ran downstairs and out into the garden.

He was in prison.

Prison was where Dad put criminals.

Prison was where the man who attacked Mary-Jane was.

'Rebecca,' Dad shouted from an upstairs window, 'don't go far. We've got to leave soon.'

Bracken wasn't a real criminal, though. His letter made perfect sense. Looking back even I could see he should've been suspicious. But hindsight was useless now.

He hadn't done anything terrible. He'd just made a mistake.

I circled round the house trying to get used to it. Bracken was in prison. I repeated it to myself as I walked past the shed, through the rose garden, under the willow, to the end of the path where Mum's apple tree was and then back round the house again.

I kept saying it until I'd said it so many times that it almost felt natural. It was just where he was. Lots of people went to prison for things they didn't mean to do. It wasn't the end of the world.

In fact, it could have been so much worse. I should've been grateful.

Bracken wasn't dead.

He hadn't been in a horrible car crash.

He hadn't left me for someone else.

He still loved me.

He was just in jail.

No wonder Stella had been so mean the last time I'd seen her. She must've blamed me. 'Miss La-di-da', she'd called me. Bracken had taken on the job to provide for me. Which to her meant that he was in prison because of me. And maybe she was right. He wouldn't have done it if I didn't exist.

And while he'd been rotting inside what had I been doing? Slowly loosening the bond between us until I could imagine a future without him. And here I was about to go and swan round Europe while he was locked in a cell.

The grass was still damp with a silvery web of dew. I sat down at the foot of Mum's apple tree, took the letter out and read it three more times. He hadn't left me. He didn't even know I'd lost the baby.

From the back door, Dad shouted, 'Rebecca, hurry up. You've got half an hour to finish packing.'

What would Mum say if she were here? She'd chosen love. Did she regret it? What was it she'd said to me before she left? 'If you don't leap, you'll never find out whether you can fly.'

But then which way was the leap? Towards Bracken or towards the new life I'd got mapped out?

I held the letter against my cheek.

Bits of wet grass stuck to the soles of my bare feet. I scraped them off and tried to imagine Bracken was there in front of me, grinning his lopsided grin, his moss-brown eyes drilling into me. I thought of the night we met, how we danced for the first time; how our bodies melted together; how I followed him barefoot into the car park and how he leant me against his van and kissed me for the first time under a starlit sky.

I imagined the weight of him pressing against me, I imagined his arms holding me, lowering me gently back onto the grass. I imagined my fingers clutching his thick dark hair, him fumbling to unfasten my jeans and then the gasp as he entered me.

'Cuppa?'

I opened my eyes to see Nat poking his head out of the shed.

'Kettle's just boiled, so I've made you one anyway.'

He ambled over and rested a steaming mug of tea beside me. Then he sat himself down cross-legged in front of me.

'Penny for them,' he said. I noticed his feet were bare too.

'You wouldn't understand. But thanks for the tea.'

'You never know. Try me.'

I looked at Nat. His hazel eyes said trust me. Then as if he could read my mind he said, 'I can keep a secret. Promise.'

Everything tumbled out.

Nat just nodded like he understood, like nothing could shock him. I told him about the pregnancy and about how Bracken had just disappeared without trace. I even told him what Pen said to me in the pub about how Bracken might be the attacker. As I told him, I realized that some small part of me had begun to believe it was a possibility.

'I feel horrible. I'm the worst human being who's ever lived. Bracken's in prison right now. It's all my fault.'

He shook his head. 'Hardly. How old was this bloke anyway?'

'That's not the point. It's not about age, it's about whether your souls match and ours did and now he's locked up and it's all my fault.'

'We all have choices.'

'Exactly. He chose love, he did what he thought love needed him to do, because he thought I wanted him to have more money.'

'And? Was he so wrong?' Nat waved his arm at the shed, the gardens and the house beyond.

'I believe in love. You don't need anything more than that.'

'Sounds like you've been listening to too many Beatles songs. *Love is all you need. Love, love, love*,' Nat sang.

'Don't laugh at me.' I stood up.

'Don't go, I'm sorry. Was just trying to get a smile out of you. I believe in love too, I just don't think it only happens once.'

'Maybe in your world,' I said and walked back to the house.

Chapter 48

I took Bracken's letter and zipped it into the inside pocket of my shoulder bag. In the drawer of my bedside table I found a photo of myself. It was old, from before I met Bracken when my hair was short, but it was the only one I could find. I didn't think he would mind. From inside my washbag I fished out Bracken's ring and slipped it onto my wedding finger; it was the first time I'd worn it since the baby had died. Dad was already in the car honking the horn. I shoved some clothes in the backpack. I didn't care which ones any more.

'Is there any particular reason why women are always so late for trains?' Dad asked as I climbed in. 'Your mother was just the same.'

'Dad, you're being a chauvinist.'

'Just an observation of fact.'

'Can I ask you something? Something about Mum?' I said as we passed the bottom of Mary-Jane's lane.

'If you must.'

'If she came back, Dad, like walked into the house or rang you or something, what would you do?'

Dad shook his head. He turned the indicator on to overtake the car in front.

'And what about what she'd done? Would you be able to forgive her?'

'Rebecca, can we not have this conversation now when we're late and I'm driving?'

We drove on in silence.

At the lights we had to wait for a mum pushing a baby in a pram to cross. That could have been me. A wave of shame swept over me as I remembered how I'd screamed at Bracken when I told him I was pregnant; how I told him he needed money and a savings account if he wanted us to have a chance.

I remember how Bracken insisted I was never to go without because of him; how he didn't want me living a life of regret; how proud he was when he got the Coventry job. How he got the job to please me.

If he hadn't got that stupid job he'd still be here now and so would the baby and soon it would be us pushing a pram together.

It was as if a dam had burst. Dad had started talking about safety and how to change money while travelling but my mind was awash with memories of all the times I must've made Bracken feel he wasn't good enough for me. I was always teasing him about how he spoke or how bad his table manners were. I never even gave him the chance to meet Dad. Then there was the house with the pillars – I knew he'd taken it to heart when I'd said I wanted to live there. I must've made him feel like he wasn't good enough. I didn't mean any of it.

I was only playing, pretending, imagining. All I ever really wanted was him.

At the station I kissed Dad's bald head goodbye and grabbed my rucksack from the boot of the car. Dad stood there stiffly, looking like he wanted to give me a hug but didn't quite dare. I flung my arms around him.

'Love you, Dad,' I said, suddenly realizing it was the first time I'd hugged him since I was little.

'I love you too,' I heard him say as I rushed into the ticket hall.

Pen and her mum would already be on the platform waiting for me. We were to catch the fast train to London where Pen's big sister would meet us and from there we'd take another one to Dover to catch the ferry. I had my passport in a little pouch hanging around my neck together with traveller's cheques and cash for hotel rooms and food.

The station had two entrances. Dad had dropped me at the front one, by the phone box. He watched from the car while I queued up to buy my ticket and gave a little toot of the horn as a final goodbye as I walked up the steps and out of sight.

At the top of the stairs there was a long raised corridor leading to the back entrance. All the way along it were steps down to each platform.

I had to make a choice.

I could go and catch the train.

Or I could just keep walking straight out through the back entrance.

I could take the money and go and live with Stella. While

I waited there for Bracken I could help her get the house straight, scrub it all clean, and maybe together we could find a way of making some money from the dogs. I'd be able to take my A levels. She might still swop bedrooms with us like she said she would and one day I'd get pregnant again and this time the baby would survive. I pictured the fields that lay to the rear of her house and felt a sense of freedom and peace. I could paint a mural of mountains and birds and the sunset a bit like the one Mary-Jane's mum had painted on her bedroom door. We could make it a real home.

It was funny how many things you could think about in a split second. Time wasn't steady and even, like the tick of a clock. It was much more elastic than that. Some seconds stretched longer than all the hours that had gone before.

This was going to be my choice. It was about who I was and what I believed in. Up until this point in my life I'd been fol-lowing a path that had been chosen for me by others. Now I got to choose my own. I thought of Tess of the D'Urbervilles and how she chose her beloved Angel even when the price was death.

Dad had been so much happier lately. He wasn't the ogre I'd always thought of him as. All he wanted was for me to do well and become an independent professional working woman so I'd always be able to provide for myself and I'd never get bored and restless and need to turn everything upside down like Mum had. But then, that was *his* version of what Mum did. I still wondered whether he just hadn't loved her enough. Hadn't made her happy. Why would she have needed to leave if she'd been really loved?

I could be happy living with Bracken and his mum. I loved the chaos and the greyhounds and the TV we could watch whenever we felt like it. I thought of Bracken's brown sheets and Stella bringing us tea in bed in the morning and the simplicity of being loved. Of it being like the sun rising and setting, something that could be depended upon. I remembered how I felt when I thought it had gone.

I stopped at the steps that led down to the platform. Pen was standing there with her mum. She had her back to me and was looking in the direction that the London train would come from. She'd got her hair in two neat plaits, so she wouldn't need to worry about washing it for ages.

They hadn't seen me.

I paused for a moment and looked down the corridor to the opening at the end. Then I heard the announcement that the London train was approaching.

It was simple. One choice, one leap that would decide everything.

Down on the platform, Pen and her mum checked their watches as the train hissed to a stop. I could imagine them asking each other where I was and wondering what I'd do if I missed the train. I glanced back to the exit that would take me to Bracken's house.

My feet were glued to the ground at the top of the stairs. Halfway down an old lady dressed smartly in a checked fawn jacket and dark navy skirt was dragging a suitcase. She was wearing low black patent shoes with gold buckles. Her brown leather suitcase was too big for her to manage and there was a bang and a small 'oh no', as it slipped from her grasp and clattered its way down the last few steps and onto the platform.

Pen's mum had opened the train door and Pen was looking desperate. A guard picked up the old lady's bag and carried it for her to the First Class carriage at the front of the train. Through a loudspeaker a clipped male voice announced that the London train was now ready to depart. Pen and her mother climbed up into the carriage.

'All aboard,' shouted the guard, slamming the door shut.

My legs started to move. I let them. I tried not to think about what I was doing. I just let them move beneath me and tried not to look back.

Becs' Top Thirty
Compilation Tape

1. 'You're My First, My Last, My Everything' – Barry White
2. 'Imagine' – John Lennon
3. 'You Sexy Thing' – Hot Chocolate
4. 'Hi Ho Silver Lining' – Jeff Beck
5. 'Brown Sugar' – Rolling Stones
6. 'Nights in White Satin' – Moody Blues
7. 'Space Oddity' – David Bowie
8. 'Hold Me Close' – David Essex
9. 'Angie Baby' – Helen Reddy
10. 'Make Me Smile (Come Up and See Me)' – Steve Harley & Cockney Rebel
11. 'One of These Nights' – The Eagles
12. 'Love Machine' – The Miracles
13. 'I'm Mandy Fly Me' – 10cc
14. 'American Pie' – Don McLean

15. 'December, 1963 (Oh, What a Night)' – Four Seasons
16. 'In The Year 2525' – Zager and Evans
17. 'Oh You Pretty Things' – David Bowie
18. 'Me and Bobby McGee' – Grateful Dead
19. 'Nutbush City Limits' – Ike and Tina Turner
20. 'Lay Lady Lay" – Bob Dylan
21. 'I Got You Babe' – Sonny and Cher
22. 'Love on a Mountain Top' – Robert Knight
23. 'I Say a Little Prayer' – Aretha Franklin
24. '(If Paradise Is) Half as Nice' – Amen Corner
25. 'Hold on to Love' – Peter Skellern
26. 'Desperado' – Eagles
27. 'I'm Not in Love' – 10cc
28. 'Seasons in the Sun' – Terry Jacks
29. 'All You Need is Love' – The Beatles
30. 'Everything I Own' – Bread

Acknowledgements

A whole host of people helped give birth to this book. First, my agent, Caroline Wood, without whose brilliance, patience and faith *Pretty Thing* wouldn't exist. Next Sarah Castleton at Constable & Robinson, who has been the most supportive and insightful editor one could wish for. Also, Tamsin Shelton for excellent editing and keeping it anchored in 1976.

My extraordinary teachers, especially Gillian Slovo at the Faber Academy and Ardashir Vakil at Goldsmiths.

Thank you to *Pretty Thing*'s early readers: Rafaella Barker, Rosie Boycott, Aly Flind, Zsuzsa Magyar, Eva Magyar, Francis Spufford and Jackson Wilson. And also to my beloved and talented writers' group, which sprang from the Faber Academy: Christopher Bland, Phillip Brady, Mark Huband, Elen Lewis, Robert Royston, Charlotte Sinclair, Imogen Sutton, Debby Turner, Katherine Wharton.

Friends, writers and guides who've helped me along the way include: Mel Agace, Charlotte Atkinson, Jim Cox, James Chambers, Rebecca Frayn, Maggie Hamand and the writers at the CCWC, John Irwin, Susannah Kleeman, Kat Lewis, Angela Martin, Tessa McWatt, Sophie Molins, Blake Morrison, Carmel Murphy, Bella Pollen, Milly St Aubyn, Pearl and Les Stace, Virginia Center for the Creative Arts, Susannah Wright and Stephanie Young.

My sons have gifted me an in-house troop of teen advisers who've shown me that, while the perils are still the same, self-awareness has thankfully rocketed. A special mention to: Lotte and Otto Brigham, Chloe Delanney, Saul and Jake Emmerson, Gabriela Lopez, Livvy Magyar, Cordelia Nagle; Stephen, Rachel and Andy Pierce; Lizzie Quacquarelli and, most importantly, Jack and Theo Wilson.

Love always and thanks to my sisters, Alison Nagle and Deborah Nadel, for their advice on this and the whole messy business of life, and also to my mother, Elizabeth Gordon.

Last but never least, thanks to Andrew for insisting I kept writing, for being my partner in this life and for so much else that is wonderful besides.